The Doctor's Dog

The Doctor's Dog

A DEAN CELLO MYSTERY

RICHARD F. VENTI

The Doctor's Dog

Published by Wheatmark®
610 East Delano Street, Suite 104
Tucson, Arizona 85705 U.S.A.
www.wheatmark.com

Publisher's Cataloging-In-Publication Data
(Prepared by The Donohue Group, Inc.)

Venti, Richard F.
The doctor's dog : a Dean Cello mystery / by Richard F. Venti.

p. ; cm.

ISBN: 978-1-58736-826-4

1. Private investigators—Massachusetts—Boston—Fiction. 2. Dogs—Fiction. 3. Mystery fiction. I. Title.

PS3622.E68 D63 2007
813.6 2007923916

Chapter 1

It was one of those rainy April afternoons when you have to remind yourself that better days are on the way. Nicole was three hundred miles away, up in Aroostook County, Maine, doing a segment on the dying timber industry in northern New England. It was now Friday and she'd been gone since Wednesday morning. I hated to admit it, but even though we'd been together for only seven months now, I seemed to have already forgotten how to enjoy myself without her.

The sports section of the *Boston Globe* offered little solace. The Sox had dropped three of their first four games of the new season. We'd waited all winter. And they'd looked so good in spring training. But what's another eighty-six years.

After sighing and reminding myself that there were a hundred and fifty-eight games left to go, I folded up the paper and placed it down on the table lamp beside the brown leather recliner in which I was seated. Then I got up briefly to microwave what was left of my coffee before returning to my favorite chair, where I sipped and listened to the patter of the rain.

Between the droplets sliding down the window of my humble study, I could see the top halves of the passersby—slickers, trench coats, hats, and umbrellas. They moved quickly, and from where I sat, silently.

What is it about the rain that makes a person think? It had now been over a year and a half since I'd quit teaching and opened shop as a private investigator. I had done so at the urging of my oldest and best friend, detective Sergeant Peter Perry of Boston's Finest. That was arguably the only good piece of advice Peter had ever given me. It wasn't that he didn't always mean well; rather, it was simply that, with his police work being the single notable exception, Peter seemed to have a great deal of difficulty taking the world and anything in it too seriously. But he was undeniably a friend in the true sense of the word. For how much longer I wasn't sure, though. He was getting married in October. Why not? Like myself, he was going on thirty-two.

My mind drifted back over the past year and a half—a series of cases involving cheating spouses, deadbeat dads, and a few missing persons. Of the whole lot of them, there was only one…

The phone startled me. I jumped up, lifted the receiver and identified myself. "Cello."

"Is this Dean Cello, Private Investigations, Discreet Inquiries?" The voice was that of a male who was obviously reading out of the phone book.

"This is Dean. How may I help you?"

"Well for starters, Mr. Cello, you could pardon my ignorance. I've never hired a private investigator before." He spoke slowly and I could hear his smile. Despite his proclamation of ignorance, he sounded relaxed and self-confident.

"Most of my clients are first-timers," I assured him. "It's that kind of business." I made sure that *my* smile too was evident.

"Very kind of you, Mr. Cello…"

"Please, call me Dean."

"Okay, Dean. Well I suppose the problem I have would best fall into the missing persons category." I waited for more and after a brief pause he continued. "I live in Lynnfield. Would it be possible for you to drive out to my home?"

The more common practice was to have clients drive in to see me in my first floor Back Bay condo unit—odd side of Beacon Street between Berkley and Clarendon. I briefly considered my rather somber mood and decided it would do me well to get out. A quick check of my watch revealed that it was quarter past two. Lynnfield was about fifteen miles north of the city off Route 1. "How about three o'clock?"

My potential client identified himself as Connor Bradley and gave me directions to his home in the prestigious Sherwood Forest section of the town.

I replaced my jeans with a pair of khakis, threw on a lightweight jacket and was out the door.

The midnight blue Z4 roadster was almost two years old now. It had been a conscious part of my metamorphosis, and while I still wasn't convinced that it suited me, it somehow did indeed now feel comfortable.

One caller after another on the sports talk station railed about the Red Sox—the questionable moves management had made in the off season, the free agents that got away. Halfway across the Mystic River Bridge I couldn't take it anymore and switched over to NPR—a piece on prize-winning dahlias. I turned off the radio and rode in silence.

Lynnfield is an affluent bedroom community and Sherwood Forest is its most exclusive section. Mr. Bradley's directions were impeccable and within minutes I spotted the large magnolia in full bloom about thirty feet behind the curbside mailbox. Its blossoms seemed incongruous in the driving rain. I motored slowly up the driveway and marveled at the large white English Tudor with three-car garage attached.

A white portico kept me reasonably dry while I waited for someone to respond to the doorbell.

Only a few seconds had passed when a conventionally handsome, blue-eyed, light-haired, mid-fifties-looking man opened the door and extended his hand. He was dressed in pleated khakis and a hunter green V-neck cashmere sweater. "Connor Bradley," he declared. "Nice of you to come out here in the rain." His handshake was firm, but not overpowering; his smile seemed genuine. He looked every bit as relaxed as he had sounded on the phone.

Mr. Bradley led me through a foyer and a large living room into a spacious and handsomely appointed study. I considered that I might want to start referring to my own study as a den. Perhaps even a nest. He gestured an invitation for me to be seated in one of the two burgundy, leather wingchairs positioned on opposite sides of a lighted fieldstone fireplace. Of course I accepted the invitation.

"Can I get you something to drink?" he asked before seating himself.

A cup of black coffee would have been my first choice, but I assumed he had something else in mind. Although I felt neither the need nor the desire to drink alcohol at the moment, I'd learned that it was usually advantageous to do whatever might make a potential client feel comfortable. "Do you by chance happen to have any amaretto?" I asked.

"I certainly do," he replied triumphantly. "On the rocks?"

"If you would please. Thank you."

Mr. Bradley walked over to a bar in the far corner of the room, and a moment later returned with my amaretto in one hand and what appeared to be a half drunk cup of coffee in the other. I managed to hide my amusement. He sat in the other chair and, after taking a sip of his coffee, smiled before asking, "So for how long have you been a private investigator?"

I was about to be interviewed. It happened sometimes. At least he seemed pleasant enough, not at all condescending, as were some of the others I'd met.

"About a year and a half now," I told him. "I used to be a high school science teacher."

His eyes widened. "Really!" he said. "I'm somewhat of a man of science myself. Although there are some who would dispute that, I'm sure."

"Oh?" I casually queried. "What is it that you do?"

"I'm a doctor," he stated matter-of-factly. "But please

don't call me Doctor, or Mr. Bradley for that matter. I prefer Connor if you don't mind."

"Than Connor it is." I couldn't resist. "So for how long have you been a doctor?"

"Touché, Dean," he declared before laughing. "I like you already."

His laugh was genuine and I couldn't help but laugh some myself.

He took another sip of coffee. "Going on thirty years, to answer your question. My son Kevin, he's the oldest of two, is now working with me and I'm about to turn the practice over to him."

"You look awfully young to be hanging it up," I said, leaving the question implied.

"I'll be turning sixty in June," he said. "Kevin just graduated from Loyola Medical last year. He's a good lad and I feel fortunate that he wants to take over the practice. Not only because I get to pass it down, but also because there's a need for family medicine these days. Seems every kid out of med school wants to be a specialist or a surgeon now." He paused to take another sip of coffee, then smiled again before continuing. "I've got patients who I've known since they were teenagers. Now I'm starting to see their children's children. It's a personal thing. I like thinking my own son will be caring for them. In a way, it's like I'll still have them."

I found myself smiling back at him admiringly. He was for real. "Is your practice right here in Lynnfield?"

"Mm-hmm. Just a couple of miles away, down in the center." He put his cup down on the table beside the chair, smiled pleasantly, and cocked his head a bit. "But enough about me," he said. "I'm interested in what makes a teacher become a PI."

I owed him and I didn't mind anyway. Besides, I'd just about had the whole spiel memorized verbatim at this point. I explained how in the idealistic naïveté of my youth I had entertained the notion of molding young minds, having a strong positive influence. What more noble cause existed? Over the course of the nine years, though, I'd learned that it wasn't knowledge that the vast majority of kids wished to acquire, it was simply the ability to make money.

"Ah, so you don't like money," the doctor said. "Then I'll assume your services are free."

I repaid the touché and we laughed again. I told him I'd grown.

"All kidding aside, Dean," he started, "and of course you don't have to answer this if you don't want to, but it must have been awfully difficult for you to establish yourself as an investigator when you didn't even have the benefit of a teacher's salary."

I explained that I'd been an only child, and that during my fourth year of teaching, both my parents had been killed in an automobile accident while returning from their summer place on Lake Winnipesaukee in New Hampshire. I thereafter couldn't bear to be in either house, so I sold them both and invested the proceeds in the stock market at what ended up turning out to be the right time.

The doctor looked at me approvingly. "You're okay, Dean. I like you," he said. "Most notably, you're honest. It's a quality that's becoming hard to find. Don't lose it."

He rose from his chair and walked over to a large mahogany desk positioned in front of the wall adjacent to the bar. He then opened a drawer and removed what from a distance appeared to be a photograph. "This is who I want you to find," he said as he closed the drawer. He began walking toward me while explaining. "His name is Sir Cedric of Winchester. He's about two feet, five inches tall and weighs sixty-four pounds." He handed me the photograph. "Of course if you don't want to accept the job I understand, but I'm willing to pay you whatever you say, within reason."

Sir Cedric was black and tan, stood on four legs, and was hairier than a Sicilian.

"An Airedale, I believe."

"You know your dogs, Dean. That's a good start."

I looked up at the doctor. He was smiling, but at the same time I could tell that he was quite serious.

"Doctor… Connor, you seem like a nice guy but… well, forgive me, but do you have any idea what the services of a private investigator cost?"

"He's not just a dog, Dean, he's a champion. From a long line of champions. And it might sound silly, but he's also my pal. I miss him. And I'm worried about him."

"And of course you've already reported his absence to the local animal control folks?"

"Of course."

I told Doctor Bradley what my usual fee was and warned that even if I agreed to accept the assignment, I couldn't guarantee success. It was unlikely that Sir Cedric had a social security number, a driver's license, a credit card, or even a post office box. It was equally unlikely that he'd ever done hard time or served in the military or been otherwise pawprinted.

While walking back toward the desk, the good doctor tried to assure me that he was very much aware that the task he wished to entrust unto me was not an easy one. He sat at the desk, and as he was still talking, I could see that he was writing out a check. He returned with both the check and several pieces of paper he'd taken from the top of the desk. He handed me the entire package.

I made note of the sizable amount of the check, placed it on the end table beside my chair, and looked over the papers—Sir Cedric's pedigree, his veterinary records, and a typed history that began with the breeder from which the dog had been purchased and ended with the last show, the one in which the beast had achieved championship status.

As I finished perusing the papers, I was still undecided. I

needed more information. The doctor had reseated himself in the chair by the fireplace. I looked over at him.

"How long has he been missing for?"

"Since Tuesday," he said. "Three days ago. I'm down to only fifteen hours a week at the office now—one to six on Mondays, Tuesdays, and Thursdays. He was here in the house when I left for work and Ellen, my wife, had a hair appointment at two. She returned home before I did, around four-fifteen, and found him gone."

"You do have a security system?"

"Mm," he muttered pensively. "Here's where it really gets interesting. Ellen says she activated the system when she left and it was still set when she returned."

I felt a bit apprehensive about asking the next question but I had to know the answer. "Who else has the code?"

"My two sons, my daughters-in-law, and my nephew Brian. Brian's the one who uses it most often. He likes Cedric almost as much as I do. Whenever Ellen and I go away, Brian takes care of the dog."

"And the two sons are your only children?"

He nodded a yes.

"Maid? Housekeeper?"

"We have a couple of women who come in once a week on Thursdays, but Ellen lets them in and out or leaves the system disarmed before they arrive."

"You haven't told me anything about your other son," I noted.

"You're right, I haven't," he acknowledged. "I guess it just didn't come up. Kevin, the doctor, is thirty-two, and Tim just turned thirty last month."

Connor Bradley went on to explain that his younger son, Tim, was a pharmacist and was married to Jill, an artist. They had one child, a three-year-old girl named Hannah. Kevin was married as well, to a bookstore proprietor named Carol. Kevin and Carol did not yet have any children.

I took notes that included where each of the family members lived and worked. If I accepted the job, I'd undoubtedly end up having a conversation with each of them.

"And obviously you've already checked with the neighbors." One could never be too sure.

"Of course," he said. "Nothing."

We sat for a moment looking at one another.

I liked Dr. Connor Bradley, but to be totally honest, it was probably the challenge that interested me most. This one would definitely be different. And I'd already been paid an advance in excess of what I would have normally required.

"I'll do my very best to find your dog, Connor."

"Wonderful," was his reply. He seemed pleased but not terribly surprised.

I pocketed the check and, with papers in hand, stood up to solidify our arrangement with a handshake. I'd just come to my feet when the doorbell rang.

"Please don't leave yet," the doctor urged. "I'll be right back."

A moment later he reentered the room with a young man whom I figured to be about college age. "Dean, this is my nephew Brian."

Brian looked like a Bradley, although his hair was darker than that of his uncle and he was smaller in stature. As we shook hands, I noticed that he was probably a couple of inches under my five foot eleven.

"Dean, I'd like it if you could stay for just a few more minutes," urged Dr. Bradley. "You see it was Brian who suggested I retain your services. Unless of course you must be getting along?"

I was going to have to speak to Brian anyway. No time like the present.

"What's a few more minutes," I said. I sat back down again; the doctor and his nephew did the same.

"Brian is a teacher," Connor informed me with a smile.

He then looked at Brian and explained that I too had been a member of that noble profession for nine years.

"Really!" Brian exclaimed, obviously surprised. He asked me which subjects I had taught and I told him biology, chemistry, and physics at the high school level. He explained that he was just finishing up his first year—elementary history and social studies in nearby Danvers. We engaged in several minutes of conversation about teaching in general. When an opportunity finally presented itself, I asked Brian if he had any theories concerning Sir Cedric's sudden disappearance.

"Not a clue," he came back. "I had classes all day on Tuesday. I only learned of it when Uncle Connor called to ask if I had him."

When Brian finished speaking, he continued to look at me. Then he smiled knowingly, and finally decided to share his secret, albeit with what I thought to be some apprehension. "I chose you out of the phone book based solely upon your name," he said. "I play the bass." He shrugged. "You know… the lows." He immediately appeared to have wished he hadn't said it, but managed an awkward chuckle.

"I hate to disappoint you," I told him, "but family legend has it that it was actually *U*cello. Supposedly the Department of Immigration lost the U somewhere."

"Close enough," he came back. "Besides it's Cello now and that's all that matters." Dr. Bradley and I laughed some, which might have encouraged Brian to make yet another comment. "If you don't mind me saying so, you don't look all that Italian. Light brown hair, green eyes…"

"Another family legend has it that my mother was half Irish," I told him.

That got them both going. The elder Bradley came back with, "I knew we had the right man."

I took advantage of the frivolity to come to my feet and initiate a smooth escape. As I did so, I noticed the amaretto that I'd placed down on the table and subsequently forgotten about. I apologized to the doctor who dismissed the idea with a quick backhanded wave. He reached out for a final handshake and then began escorting me to the door. As he did so, Brian told him that he too had to be leaving; he'd just stopped by to meet Mr. Cello.

Dr. Bradley bid us both a good evening and I assured him I'd be in touch. When he opened the door, I noticed that the rain had finally stopped.

"I was admiring your car on the way in," Brian said. "Can I get a look inside?"

"Yeah, sure," I casually agreed. "When I first got it I wasn't sure it suited me. Sometimes I still think the real me is the boxy old Volvo I traded in for it." What I didn't want to tell him was that I had made a conscious effort to shed the teacher image. "But now it's become comfortable," I added. "I've grown attached to it."

I opened the driver's side door and Brian leaned over some, apparently to get a closer look inside. As he did so he quietly muttered, "Can you meet me around ten o'clock tomorrow morning at Lou's Donut Shop on Main Street?" He stood back up and, smiling, pointed toward the dashboard while saying, "I think you'll find what I have to tell you rather interesting." Obviously, he was trying to appear nonchalant just in case his uncle was still watching from the window.

Okay, I'll play along. I pointed at the same dashboard, nodded and said, "I can do that."

He took a step backward and, still smiling, slowly looked the car over admiringly from the front bumper to the rear and then back again. "And don't worry," he said. "I've got the dog."

Chapter 2

It was twenty minutes past six when I parked the car along the Revere seawall, crossed the boulevard, and walked into High Tide. I was supposed to meet Peter at six-thirty, but it was no surprise to find him already there, a beer in one hand, unlit cigarette in the other. While it was true that he was sometimes uncouth, often sophomoric, it had to be acknowledged that he was always punctual. Donned in a maroon sweatshirt and faded jeans, he was seated in his usual spot at the bar, looking up at the TV. I got the bartender's attention and asked for a glass of Chianti before I sat down.

Peter turned to notice me and smiled through his thick, black, walrus mustache. "How's it going, pal?"

"Not bad at all. In fact I just picked up a new case. Lynnfield."

"Anything interesting?"

"I'm not sure." I thought for a moment. "I don't think so."

He looked at me, waiting for more.

"A doctor hired me to…" It occurred to me that I was in danger of subjecting myself to one of his infantile spasms of laughter. I sighed. "You know, it's so boring I don't even want to talk about it. So what's new with you?"

He slowly turned his muscular torso to face me and rested his forearm on the back of the barstool. For a few seconds, he just nodded and smiled knowingly. "Well, haven't we become the pompous one," he finally said. "Was it not just two years ago that you were in a funk about having become a boring bastard…" He pointed a finger at me. "Your words… And I had to expend vast quantities of energy to convince you that it might do you good to quit teaching—"

"Yes, yes. I owe it all to you, old friend." My wine arrived as if on cue. I raised it toward him and we clanked glass to bottle. Before he took a swallow, he got out a low, "You bet your ass you do."

As was our usual custom, we moved to a small table and ordered some of what was arguably the best seafood on the North Shore. Peter had fried clams and a box of onion rings; I chose the scallops and pier fries.

After eating a couple of the fries, I casually commented, "These are still the best anywhere. If it weren't for all the fat, I'd definitely have them more often."

Peter studied me for a moment. I could tell it was going to be special. "I remember hearing somewhere that when the Iroquois found out that the white man was trying to make the wolf extinct, they took that as proof that he was insane."

I looked at him. "And exactly how did we get there from here just now?"

"You worrying about what you're eating," he said. "The Iroquois were right. Nature has a plan. You can't fight it."

"And the plan is for me to die before I have to?"

"Kind of. That's why everything that tastes good is bad for you and everything that tastes bad is good for you. You're only supposed to live long enough to reproduce. After that, Nature wants you to get out of the way."

"So you feel the wise course of action is to help Nature kill you sooner rather than later."

"Exactly. That way I never have to worry about it."

I was never sure, so I usually just left those alone.

I overheard somebody at a nearby table mention the Red Sox. Although Peter and I were decidedly different personality-wise, we had since high school shared a love for both baseball and the blues, those being the common threads that had originally brought us together. And by now, of course, we also shared a lot of great memories as well.

"So are you still as optimistic about the Olde Towne Team as you were a couple of weeks ago?" I asked.

I posed the question just as he was beginning to take another swallow of beer. Rather than wait in silence, I took the liberty of filling in for him by offering my own opinion. "I suppose they still look pretty decent on paper. Strong up the middle. Good power from the right side. They could probably use a left-handed bat off the bench, though. And a middle reliever wouldn't hurt either."

Peter's analysis was more succinct. "They suck," he said.

Apparently four games were enough for him. Or at least until they'd won a few. He changed the subject.

"Seriously," he implored in his heavy baritone, "tell me about your new case."

"Ah, why not?" I said. "I've been hired to find a lost dog."

He had just begun to take another drink, and albeit not by design, my timing was perfect. He lurched forward suddenly, beer spewing forth from his nose. Minus the beer part, I'd seen this before. He'd remain silent in that forward-leaning position with his eyes closed and that shit-eating grin on his face for approximately five full seconds, then he'd emit a single prolonged howl followed by a rapid succession of cackles that in the end would leave him gasping for air. Every time I witnessed it, I had the same thought—*They let him carry a gun.* The howl portion of the event was always accompanied by wide eyes, and in this instance, it was enhanced by the beer dripping from his walrus mustache. As usual, the performance garnered a fair amount of attention from other patrons who had the misfortune of being seated nearby. Also as usual, I tried to appear casual and relaxed. Maybe they'd think I was his psychiatrist.

When Peter had sufficiently collected himself, I explained that Sir Cedric was a champion. I also expounded about what a down-to-earth nice guy the doctor seemed to be and how, despite the seemingly unimportant nature of the case, I found it interesting because of the challenge it presented. I was saving the nephew part for last.

"Challenge my ass," said Peter.

"What am I missing?" I asked rhetorically. "It's a missing 'person' with no social security number, no driver's license, no credit card, no arrest record, and no fingerprints. What would *you* do?"

"Just buy another dog," he said.

Obviously, he wasn't serious and I saw no point in encouraging him. I told him about the nephew thing at the end of my visit with Dr. Bradley. Hopefully, tomorrow morning I'd have a better idea of what was going on.

As was usually the case, Peter had for the most part tired of himself and become almost normal by the time we'd finished our second round. As serious as ever about his work, he gave me what Nicole's Channel 3 news didn't about a double murder that had taken place in the South End. Then he reiterated how well he got along with his future father-in-law, a retired cop who'd worked in the North Shore town of Winthrop, where Peter and his fiancée Linda had recently bought a house. Peter and Frank had gone fishing last Saturday up on Sebago.

I recalled aloud that I hadn't been fishing since my father took me out on Winnipesaukee back when I was ten years old.

"Why don't you join us sometime?" Peter suggested.

"You know, I just might—"

"It's a plan!" he said. "Next time Nicole's out of town and you don't have a dog to not find, we'll hit one of the lakes up in New Hampshire. I know a few great spots."

I nodded my agreement and obligingly met his bottle with my empty glass. He drank for both of us.

"So how does it feel to be getting married in six months?" I asked.

"Great," he responded without hesitation.

I could tell that he meant it. It felt strange.

"Linda's perfect for me," he continued quite seriously. "She knows who I am and she accepts me totally. Not to mention that I'm crazy in love with her."

"Meaning you're crazy and you're in love with her."

"Yeah, that too." He emitted a hint of a laugh. He never denied his insanity; he seemed to be genuinely proud of it.

"What's it been now… about three years?"

"Almost four," he stated proudly.

I nodded. "Seriously, I give you credit. I never thought I'd see it."

"Yeah," he said rather sheepishly. It wasn't like him to be lost for words and he must have felt it too. "So how long have you been with Nicole now?"

I was sure he hadn't meant it to come out the way it did, so I played it straight. "Seven months. Since September."

The barmaid came over and asked if she could get us another round. Peter readily agreed to another beer. Instead of more wine, I opted for the coffee I hadn't asked for at Dr. Bradley's house.

When the barmaid left, Peter looked me straight in the eye and spoke without any hint of sarcasm. "I'm glad you found Nicole," he said. "She's a great woman. And you guys are perfect for one another."

I couldn't help but study him for a moment. He could be so juvenile, but then, unexpectedly, he could suddenly be so real.

"You're a weird bastard," I told him.

He knew what I meant and we both laughed.

"All kidding aside," he said, "I don't think I ever told you this before, but I'm really proud of you. For a while there a few years ago, when Holly first left you to marry What's His Name, I didn't think you were going to make it."

"Yeah, well, fortunately I had an old friend who was

willing to get drunk with me on more than a few occasions."

"No, seriously," he insisted. "After too. I'm sure it wasn't easy to quit a steady job and do all that had to be done to get licensed. You even moved back into the city and bought a spiffy upscale roadster."

"Tangible evidence of my metamorphosis. But since we're being so serious, in retrospect, my breakup with Holly was probably the best thing that ever happened to me. It turned out to be exactly what I needed to break free and restructure my life."

Peter nodded. "Of course you still talk like a friggin' schoolteacher."

"Thanks. I'd have been disappointed if you hadn't thrown that in, you miserable ex-jock excuse for an officer of the law."

Over the next hour or so we talked seriously about our women and our work. Peter had made an arrest in a matter that involved a guy we'd gone to high school with. Neither one of us were surprised that he'd ended up on the wrong side of the law.

Eventually, we split the check and called it a night.

As I climbed into the Z4 and started the engine, I was aware that an unsettling feeling had come over me. By the time I turned onto the Revere Beach Parkway to head back toward Boston, I realized that my uneasiness stemmed from the conversation I'd just had with Peter. For more than half my life, he had proven to be the one constant. When my parents had their tragic accident, he couldn't do enough. And then when Holly left me to marry Richard, the child psychologist, he was there for me then too. In fact he was so consistent that he hadn't even ever really grown up. I'd always complained about his sophomoric manner, so now that he was finally showing signs of making it to adulthood, why was I feeling so uneasy? It was because I was witnessing the beginning of the end, the passing of an era as it were. He'd just admitted that he was in love after having been with the same woman exclusively for almost four years. And he was about to get married. What would be next? Mowing a lawn in the suburbs? Children? Soccer games instead of High Tide. The one constant in my life was about to disappear.

I thought about Nicole. By contrast to Peter's four years, my seven months seemed puny. Would Nicole and I be together in four years? Right now it felt like it would last forever, but didn't it always feel that way after just seven months?

As I approached the Tobin Bridge, my mind drifted back to September, when Nicole and I first met. She had recently moved down to the city from Derry, New Hampshire, having started her new job doing human-interest stories for Channel 3's News of New England. She was a twenty-seven-year old journalism-communications major who had just come off an internship in Manchester, and I used to tease her about missing the cows. I'd met her on the front steps of our building just a few days after she'd moved in upstairs. Continuing to reminisce, I pictured her as she was on that weekend when I was first attracted to her—her petite form with the ocean behind her, looking up at me with those caramel eyes with the shots of olive bursting out from the center, her shortish chestnut hair blowing in the breeze, that extra clean look, that super warm smile. Was it possible that I was even wilder about her than I'd been about Holly just a few years ago? It must have been because I was sure that I was. But I was old enough to know that a lot could change after just seven months. It was way too soon to even *consider* mowing my *own* lawn in the suburbs. Besides, I was quite content to keep things just the way they were for the foreseeable future, thank you.

I shook my head clear. Dean Cello had faced adversity before and survived. More than once, in fact. What was there to be uneasy about?

I arrived home and checked my messages. I had just one; it was from Nicole. She sounded as cheerful as ever—"Hi. I miss you so much. I bet you miss me too 'cause I'm so cute. I'm going to bed early; we've got a seventy-something mile ride ahead first thing in the morning and then an interview in Holton at ten. I'll try to call again in the morning. Wish I was home with you. Goodnight."

I walked into the study still smiling, turned on the TV and picked up the ballgame in the bottom of the seventh. It was cold in Kansas City. Every player on the field was wearing the long sleeve jersey under his uniform top. The pitchers were blowing in their hands.

I watched the Sox lose six to four and then I went to bed.

Despite my heavy thinking after talking with Peter at High Tide, what I saw and heard when I first closed my eyes was young Brian Bradley. What on earth was he doing with the dog?

Chapter 3

As always, I started out the next day with my early morning run. On this occasion, I chose the alternate route—down Charles Street to Storrow Drive, around Beacon Hill, and back through the Common and the Public Gardens. On the eastern horizon, the sun was trying to break through a thin layer of cloud covering, but the sky to the west was solid blue. It looked like the rain had moved out and it was eventually going to be a beautiful day.

Upon arriving back at my condo, I showered and changed into Saturday clothes. Even though I hadn't worked a Monday through Friday job for some time now, I still made it a point to wear jeans on Saturdays whenever possible. It helped define the weekend. Besides, on this particular occasion, I figured the folks at Lou's Donut Shop wouldn't mind.

Main Street in Lynnfield is not the busy Main Street one typically thinks of. After passing a muffin shop, an electronics repair place, and a pizza house, I spotted Lou's Old Fashioned Donuts up ahead on the left.

The outside of the building looked rather typical for an establishment of its kind, but walking into the place was like stepping through a time portal. It was done in retro nineteenth century—wooden floorboards lightly sprinkled with sawdust, an ornate pale green zinc ceiling, and a potbelly stove, which at the time at least, wasn't lighted.

Although I was about five minutes early, Brian was already there, seated at a table by the window. When he saw me, he hopped up and headed over. "What are you having?" he asked.

"How about a sugared cruller and a black coffee?"

He nodded an okay. "You should probably hold the table," he suggested. "I'll be right back."

I did as Brian recommended, which in fact made sense. The place was almost filled to capacity.

When Brian returned, he hadn't yet placed the coffees and donuts down on the table when he apologized for having me drive back up from Boston. "It's just that I couldn't say too much at Uncle Connor's," he explained.

"Does he ever come in here?" I asked. We were just a few miles from his house, after all.

"You never have to worry about that," Brian said. "Breakfast is the one meal he always eats at home. Prepares it himself. Besides, he went up to New Hampshire with Kevin this morning. They're looking at some property Kevin is thinking of buying on Lake Winnipesaukee."

I nodded my understanding and took a bite of my cruller. It was an outstanding one, the exterior nice and crunchy.

Brian bit into his lemon-filled and looked back at me.

I took a sip of my coffee.

Brian did the same and again looked back.

"Well then," I said cheerfully.

Brian laughed a bit nervously, but then his expression changed to one of concern. He took a deeper than normal breath, exhaled, and then leaned in a bit closer before speaking. "The dog," he said. "You're going to think I'm terrible, but I had to do something to get Uncle Connor to hire someone. He's in danger, but he can't see it. Or more to the point, he can't admit it." His voice was trembling some; he sounded unsure of himself.

I nodded again and took another sip of coffee, giving him more time to get comfortable.

He continued. "Three Saturdays ago, I came over to have breakfast with him. I do that sometimes. Anyway, this time, he didn't answer the bell. I rang again, knocked, and then finally used my key to get in. I called for him, but he didn't answer. I went all through the house looking for him and finally found him in bed. He never sleeps that late—almost ten o'clock. Then I noticed he was all flushed. I called to him, but he didn't hear me so I started shaking him. He started to wake up a bit; he was conscious, but very groggy. I picked up the phone and hit nine one one. After I put the phone down, I kept shaking him and talking to him. Then I opened the window to get some fresh air in the room. By the time the paramedics arrived, he was starting to come out of it, but he was still far from normal. I remember as they were getting him out of the bed, he reached up and said, 'My head.' He repeated that again while they were taking him downstairs too. They gave him oxygen in the ambulance, then later, he was treated and released at Melrose General. As it turned out, he had monoxide poisoning."

When Brian stopped long enough to catch his breath, I asked the obvious question. "Did anyone figure out what had caused the monoxide poisoning?"

"The only thing they could think of was the furnace," he said. "They suggested nobody sleep there until it had been checked. I went back to crack the windows open before going home. Uncle Connor and his wife spent the next two nights at Kevin's house."

My next question was admittedly peripheral, but Brian's mention of his having gone home caused it to come to mind. "Do you live alone, Brian?"

"Yeah," he confirmed, almost apologetically.

"Danvers?"

"Yeah, I live in the Brookstone Village condo complex on Locust Street." He nodded.

I nodded too, although I had no idea where it was. "So did your Uncle Connor get the furnace checked out?"

"Monday morning," he said. Although Brian had sat back a minute ago, he now leaned in over the table again. "This is where it really gets weird," he continued. "The service guy told Uncle Connor that the chimney was congested. Said he needed to get it cleaned out. So Uncle Connor called a couple of chimney sweeps. Fortunately, he got one to come over that afternoon." Brian paused and stared at me as if for effect. "The chimney was full of dried leaves."

I stared back at him. Then I took a sip of coffee. Apparently that was it.

I tried to smile agreeably and pleaded, "Help me out here."

"Enough leaves to cause carbon monoxide to back up to the point where it became deadly?" he asked. "It was the end of March. Leaves fall in October."

I was still working on that when Brian apparently felt the need to further his theory by proffering an additional argument. "Okay, just hold that one on the shelf for a moment. There's more." He had overcome his nervousness and was now speaking with confidence.

"Before you go on," I said, "I have a question, if I may."

He raised his eyebrows and waited.

"Where was Ellen, his wife, during all this?"

"She was in New York State," he explained. "Outside of Albany. She has an older sister who's not well—lung cancer. Ellen went to stay with her for the weekend." Brian flashed a grin of satisfaction. "Pretty convenient, huh?"

Did I understand correctly? "You think your Aunt Ellen stuffed leaves in the chimney?"

"No, no," he said, waving his hand across the table. "It's just that... well at least it's possible that someone wanted to do Uncle Connor without doing Ellen."

I caught myself smiling and nodding again. "Okay," I offered.

"Alright, alright," he said as he repositioned himself in the chair. He put down the donut he'd been holding after having taken only the one bite. "As I said a minute ago, just hold that one on the shelf for a moment. There's more."

Brian noticed that I was down to my last inch of coffee. "Can I get you some more coffee, Mr. Cello?"

"I'm fine, thanks. And please, call me Dean."

"Okay," he said, and eagerly resumed. "That was three weeks ago. Now *last* week, a week ago last night to be exact, he was driving home from... Oh. Uncle Connor gets together with a few of his old doctor friends on Friday nights. Usually a card game. They've been doing it for years. Anyway, he was coming home from Dr. Golden's house in Saugus and... it was eleven-fifteen when it happened... he was driving up Route 1, and as he approached the Walnut Street overpass, someone dropped a fifty-two pound rock on his car! Or tried to at least. The rock landed just a few feet in front of him and bounced up off the grill. Naturally, he lost control for a moment, but fortunately he recovered before he hit the concrete embankment or went off the road. The front end of the Lexus was pretty badly damaged—grill, hood, ruptured radiator, something to do with the suspension too." Brian stopped abruptly and placed both palms face up on the table.

"I read about that in the paper," I told him. "But of course I didn't know it was your uncle."

This time, he nodded with his whole upper body.

"But I remember," I continued, "that the police attributed the rock to kids."

"Sure," he responded enthusiastically. "Why would they have any reason to think anything else?"

I raised my eyebrows slightly and hoped he'd realized what he'd just said. Indeed, why would *anyone* think anything else?

He seemed to get the message, but he wasn't persuaded. "Look," he said. "Even if you can somehow explain away leaves clogging up a chimney in March after it worked fine all winter, and even if you acknowledge the possibility that some crazy kids could have dropped that rock onto the highway, you still have to admit that it would be quite a coincidence for both of those things to have happened within two weeks' time."

I was thinking about that when he added, "How many close calls with death did *you* have in the past two weeks?"

We looked at one another.

"Have you presented your theory to your uncle?" I asked.

"Yeah, sure," he murmured, showing his frustration. He obviously wasn't going to elaborate without some prompting.

"So what did he have to say about it?"

Brian sunk down in his chair and stared at the table as he spoke. "He said things happen. He said thousands of coincidences occur every day. And he said that he doesn't have an enemy in the world."

After a moment, I started as cautiously as I knew how. "Well first, let me say that I think your concern for your uncle is commendable. You're obviously very close to him."

Brian closed his eyes. He could tell what was coming.

"But I'm afraid," I continued, "that I tend more to agree with the doctor on this one. The fact is that the world *is* full of coincidences. They *do* happen every day. If we tried to attach a meaning to all of them..."

Brian shook his head, then placed his elbows on the table and leaned his face into his hands.

"Look, Brian, I admit I can't say with absolute certainty that someone's not out to get your uncle. But apparently even *you* can't point a finger at anybody. It seems you *agree* that your Uncle Connor doesn't have an enemy in the world."

With his elbows still on the table, he rested his chin in his hands and stared at me.

I thought I'd try another angle. "I'm really sorry, Brian. Maybe if we had something a little more definitive—some kind of a clue, something to work with. But as it is, even if you're right, it could be any one of so many people. It could even be a patient. How many of those does he have? And you know… I hate to have to mention this, but I think you can appreciate that I'm in a rather awkward position with your uncle. He wrote me a check for a substantial amount, and as it turned out, I knew where his dog was before I even left his house."

"How did leaves that fell in October not make the chimney congested until March?" he demanded.

I thought for a moment. "We had a late season snow-storm in the second week of March," I reminded him. "The snow could have packed down leaves that had previously been loose."

Brian digested that and then shook his head, apparently rejecting it. Then he made a proposition. "I tell you what, Mr. Cello. *I'll* pay you to investigate who's trying to kill my uncle. That way you won't have to worry about having his check. Just don't deposit it and after you find out who's responsible you can give it back."

I really did admire him for his tenacity, but I couldn't take his money. "Do you have any idea how much that would cost?" I asked.

"I don't care," he snapped. "I have what I need. I don't value money that much."

For a brief moment I envied him. The innocence of youth.

I didn't know what else to offer. In an effort to get him to recognize the futility of his mission, I said, "Even if I were to agree, where would you suggest we begin?"

As soon as it was out, I knew it had sent the wrong message.

Brian grinned from ear to ear. "His wife was the one who found the dog missing," he said. "It would seem logical that you'd start there."

I didn't mean to smile, but it was too late. "Got this all figured out, have you?"

"This is great," he said. "I've got a couple of local errands to do. Can you meet me at Uncle Connor's house in a half-hour? Ellen can give you the tour."

"The tour?"

"First time anyone comes to the house, she always gives them the tour." He hadn't stop grinning yet.

What else did I have to do anyway? Maybe if he saw how difficult it was going to be, he'd accept the fact that the cause was hopeless. "In a half-hour," I said. "But no guarantees."

We left Lou's and hopped into our respective vehicles. I noticed for the second time that Brian's was a dark green Subaru Forester—practical, dependable, sensible. Yeah, and I was a stud.

As I drove out to Route 1, I recalled Shakespeare's observation about how much a man's father learns during the period of time in which the son ages from twenty to thirty.

I stopped at a local Walgreen's and picked up a few essentials I was running low on, and then drove down to neighboring Saugus. As I passed under the Walnut Street overpass, I wondered. Who knows?

Making use of the next overpass, I reversed direction and headed north, back into Lynnfield.

The Forester was in the driveway. It was safe to ring the bell.

The face that greeted me was mid-fifties, but the body could have belonged to a woman of much fewer years. Her hair was silver, blunt cut, and she was tastefully dressed in black pants and a crisp, white, man-tailored shirt. There was no doubt in my mind that the diamond studs in her ears were the real thing.

"Ah, and you must be Mr. Cello," she said rather stiffly. "Do come in."

Brian appeared and did the formal introductions, and immediately thereafter, Mrs. Bradley wasted no time in offering her opinion.

"Well I must tell you, Mr. Cello, in my own view..." She placed a hand on her heart. "I think it preposterous for the doctor to be hiring the services of a... a person of your profession to find a dog. Rather silly, wouldn't you say?" I'd barely opened my mouth when she added, "Well of course you needn't answer that. I'm sure the question places you in a most precarious position, hmm? Come. Let me show you around. You might as well get a look at the residence of the doctor who has taken you into his employ as it were."

Was she for real? "Very kind of you."

Mrs. Bradley showed me around the house while Brian waited in the doctor's study. The entire tour took about ten minutes and the Mrs. wore a frozen smile the whole time. She "introduced" me to the exercise room, the heated indoor pool, each of the bedrooms, the guest room, the dining room, and the "formal" room, which contained her "prized possession," an antique teacart—an "original Sorrento." The last place she took me to was the "recently remodeled" kitchen. I doubted that she ever cooked in it.

When the tour was completed, Mrs. Bradley dismissed me with, "Well I'm sure you gentlemen have business to attend to. I trust you can find your way back to the study."

"Thanks for having faith in me," I said, and immediately realized that I shouldn't have.

When I reentered the study, Brian was grinning broadly. "She's a piece of work, isn't she?"

I wanted to tell him that I could see why his uncle was so desperate to find the dog, but this time I caught myself. "Let's take a look at that chimney," I said instead.

The sun was now shining brightly as Brian and I descended the two steps in front of the portico and started around the corner to the far side of the house.

Brian pointed to the chimney. Somehow he seemed to remain oblivious to the woods, which in that spot was less than a hundred feet away. Roughly three-quarters of it was made up of oak.

For a moment, we stood side by side, looking at the chimney and the surrounding area.

When it seemed that Brian wasn't going to notice that the trees there still held some of their leaves, I placed a hand on his shoulder and, with the other hand, pointed to the nearby woods. How could I tell him without making him feel stupid? Maybe a little humor. "I know you do history; I'm the science guy. Do you know what kind of trees those are?"

He stared at them. "Oaks," he said.

I gave him a few more seconds.

"Why do they still have leaves?" he asked as an awkward smile started to appear.

"Oaks are rather unique," I explained. "They do lose more than half their leaves in the fall, but the rest stay on until the new buds push them off in the spring."

"I never noticed that before," he said. He turned to me, obviously a bit embarrassed, but still managing a smile.

"So how come you never helped with the spring yard work?" I joked.

"I raked in the fall and did snow in the winter," he said. "But spring meant just one thing to me—baseball."

That remark opened the door for a casual conversation. Brian had played second base for Lynnfield High School. He'd been a decent hitter for a little guy, if he did say so himself. We discussed the horrendous start the Red Sox had gotten off to, but there was still plenty of time left; maybe they'd get it together. While we were chatting, I casually led the way back to the driveway.

When the baseball conversation ended, I cuffed Brian on the shoulder and suggested, "Why don't you think about this. You've got my number, right?"

"Yeah," he said. "I guess I'm going to have to reconsider.

I hadn't noticed the trees and I also hadn't thought about the storm we had a couple of weeks ago. I suppose if you take the chimney thing away, then that just leaves the rock and… I guess without the chimney thing first… Well the rock by itself…" He shrugged. "Kids do some crazy things."

"Think it over," I repeated, as I extended my hand. "And if you should decide not to pursue this thing, think about how you're going to handle the situation with your uncle. And then be sure to call me. I've still got his check."

We shook hands and Brian thanked me for my time. He told me he'd be in touch before the weekend was out. I started for my car thinking that I'd probably never see Brian Bradley again.

There was just one call on the machine when I got home. Again, it was from Nicole. "I thought I might catch you before you left the house. I'm sure you won't have your cell on, so I'm not even going to try. We're going to be taping on and off throughout most of the day, but if you want to try me around four o'clock… Hopefully, we'll be finished by then." She sang off. "I miss you."

Four o'clock was three hours away. I fixed myself a roast beef sandwich and started watching the ballgame. By the time I finished the sandwich, the Royals had scored four runs.

I abandoned the ballgame and sat down at the computer, where I opened a new file and called it "the doctor's dog." It had become my habit to keep notes on all my cases, although in this instance, I didn't really expect this minor fiasco to become a case per se. Nevertheless, I wrote a brief page and a half, named it, saved it, and filed it away. Someday it might bring a feeble smile to a reminiscing old man.

With channel changer in hand, I stretched out on the brown leather sofa adjacent to the matching recliner.

A couple of hours later, I awoke to discover that the Sox

had squeaked out a nine to eight victory with a pinch-hit single up the middle in the top of the ninth. Two and four with a hundred and fifty-six left to play.

It wasn't quite four o'clock yet, but I thought I'd try Nicole. She answered on the second ring.

"Hi, Nicole. Dave Feldman here at Channel 3. I want you to get back to Boston right away."

"Gee, do I have to, Dave? I've got a date with this great looking lumberjack tonight."

I reverted to my normal voice. "Good for you. I've got a date with a rented movie. Or maybe a good book, if there is such a thing on a Saturday night."

"Good boy," she said with a smile I could hear.

I asked her how the job was going and she told me they had just finished up about fifteen minutes ago. It was a big enough project that Feldman was considering running it in two parts on consecutive nights.

"We'll be leaving right after breakfast," she said. "I should be home somewhere around dinner time. Where are you taking me?"

"Well if you've been up there hanging out with handsome lumberjacks for three days, I think it's clear that *you* owe *me*."

We chatted a bit more and then did our I-love-yous before I headed out the door wearing a smile made for the village idiot.

I strolled over to Copley Place and walked the mall.

Dinner consisted of Cajun chicken and rice in the food court, after which I left the mall and wondered over to Blockbuster. There I selected my evening entertainment—a Bruce Willis film, the name of which I no longer remember.

By the time I got home, there was again a single message waiting. It had arrived at 6:23. "Mr. Cello, this is Brian Bradley. I've decided not to pursue the, ah, the thing about my uncle. I've already explained the whole situation to him.

He was actually pretty happy to hear that Cedric was okay. And he, ah, well he was really flattered that I had been so concerned about him. So, anyway, if you want to call him about the money part… Well you have his number, right? Thanks again."

I watched Bruce outsmart and beat up the bad guys, and then I channel surfed for a while before settling on Saturday Night Live and eventually falling asleep on the sofa.

Sunday morning was sunny, but seasonably cool. I still needed a sweatshirt for my run. This time I took the regular route—up Beacon Street to Arlington, over the Arthur Feidler Footbridge, along the esplanade, and back via the Dartmouth Street Bridge. Nicole would be coming home this afternoon.

After showering and getting dressed, I poured myself a cup of coffee and sat in the recliner with the Sunday paper. After having read the sports page and a portion of the news, I folded up the rest of the paper, saving the Science and Health section for later.

It was still too early to call the doctor's house. I'd wait awhile and then make arrangements to return his check, hopefully in person.

I decided to take a leisurely drive up along the North Shore.

The dashboard clock read 10:08 when I pulled off Route 1A and into the parking lot of a pancake house. I punched in the doctor's number and immediately recognized the voice at the other end as that of the piece of work. "Bradley residence," she answered.

"Good morning, Mrs. Bradley. Dean Cello. May I speak to Dr. Bradley please?"

"And might I ask why you want to do that?" she inquired.

"I have something to return to him. I'd like to drop by briefly sometime today if I may."

Her response was immediate. "You shan't have to do that," she assured me. "You see, Mr. Cello, the doctor is dead."

Chapter 4

The doctor's untimely demise being a given, I might have expected "The doctor has passed away," or maybe even, from Mrs. Bradley, "The doctor is deceased." But "The doctor," my husband, "is dead." Strange to say the least.

"An unfortunate accident" was the way Mrs. Bradley responded to my inquiry as to what had happened. Under the circumstances, of course, I didn't want to press. The accidental death of a local doctor would undoubtedly be worthy of an article in the town newspaper anyway.

I thought about how I'd dismissed Brian. It might have been easy to feel guilty except that, even if I'd taken him seriously, what could I have accomplished between yesterday afternoon and this morning? Still. I had to call him.

I hit four one one and was told that there was no listing for a Brian Bradley on Locust Street in Danvers. That didn't seem all that odd, though. A lot of young people used only their cell phones these days.

I drove home asking myself the same two questions over and over again—What kind of an accident had he had? And could it be that it really was just an accident?

I decided I needed to get my mind off it. There was nothing I could do about it anyway.

Upon arriving home, I called my Aunt Lucy in the North End and told her I wanted to surprise Nicole with a dinner I prepared myself. This would be a first. Up until now my knowledge of food had been limited to how to eat it. Aunt Lucy, excited that I was finally going to use the cookware she'd bought me six years ago, gave me a recipe that she assured me even a novice couldn't screw up. Her words.

I had to go back out briefly to get a few items at the

supermarket, but the trip was relatively painless and I actually ended up with a better parking space when I returned.

I called Nicole on her cell to find out what time she'd be getting home—around 4:30. I made her promise not to eat anything and to call me when she crossed into Massachusetts.

"Got to get your other girlfriend out of the house, huh?"

"Something like that."

Without asking for an explanation, she assured me that she'd call and we disconnected.

For the next couple of hours I read the paper, primarily the Science and Health section, while more or less, mostly less, listening to the ballgame in the background.

Shortly after 3:30, the phone rang. "I'm at the Hampton toll booth. Tell that wench to get dressed."

I started broiling the Italian sausage and preparing the cream sauce for the fettuccini alfredo.

Once those tasks were completed, I set the table while the pasta was boiling. Then I poured the cabernet, lit two candles, and turned off the light over the table. Tell me I'm not a romantic bastard.

The pasta was ready about ten minutes before the bell rang—not long enough to have any deleterious effect. I hit the buzzer and went to greet Nicole at the door.

She hit me with that warm smile of hers, dropped her luggage while still in the hallway, and hugged me tightly, burying her head in my chest. I understood. It felt as though she'd been gone for a month. We were hopelessly sickening.

After a prolonged and decidedly passionate kiss, I told her, "You seem to have an awful lot left for a girl who just spent a night with a handsome lumberjack."

"He's up in Holton now. You'll have to do," she said.

I took her hand and led her to the kitchen, where dinner was about to be served in the glow of the candlelight.

Nicole sighed a heartfelt "Oh," looked at me approvingly, and gave me another hug.

While we ate dinner, Nicole filled me in on what was left of the timber industry this side of Nova Scotia—the closed mills, both lumber and paper, and the impact those closings had had on the families and businesses that for so long had depended upon them.

Nicole, in her typically upbeat fashion, offered her opinion that, despite the serious hardships the mill closings had caused, there nevertheless was a bright side too. "People who previously knew nothing but timber are now diversifying. They're finding new niches in a variety of endeavors they'd previously never imagined themselves getting involved in."

I couldn't quite stifle a chuckle.

"What?" she asked.

"You're amazing," I told her. "You could put a positive spin on a crashing asteroid."

Never to be outwitted, she replied, "Lucky for you, huh, Dino?"

Nicole assured me that my first attempt at the culinary art had been a smashing success. We sat chatting softly while intermittently swirling and sipping the wine in our glasses until at one point we found ourselves just silently staring at one another. That little smile started across Nicole's mouth—not the warm, softhearted one—the mischievous one that was accompanied by the sparkle in those caramel eyes.

We left the dishes for tomorrow.

As usual, my biological alarm clock woke me just before seven. Nicole was still sleeping; I admired her for a minute before getting up to don my shorts and sweatshirt.

Storrow Drive was backed up early—typical for a Monday

morning. Would I ever get tired of rejoicing in the fact that I had no clock to punch?

I returned from my run just after eight, and Nicole, as had been her habit for the past seven months, had already gone two flights up to her own place to take a shower. Although I could have counted the times she'd slept in her own bed since she moved into the building last September, she still went upstairs to shower every morning before coming back down for breakfast. I couldn't help but wonder if she too still needed to maintain a bit of independence.

I emerged from my own shower to find her back downstairs and preparing breakfast—French toast.

"It's not fettuccini alfredo from a world class chef, but I hope it'll do," she offered.

In fact she knew I loved her French toast. She made the edges nice and crispy and sprinkled just the right proportion of sugar and cinnamon on top. It occurred to me that I was getting spoiled.

During dinner the night before, Nicole had asked me what I'd been up to while she was away, but she seemed to be on a roll about Maine, so I told her I'd fill her in later. It was now later.

Between bites of French toast and sips of coffee, I briefly mentioned that I'd met Peter at High Tide on Friday night, and then I related the entire Dr. Bradley story complete with "The doctor is dead" and no word yet from Brian.

When I finished, Nicole seemed to have fixed on something other than the Bradleys. "Why is Peter getting married bothering you so much?" she wanted to know.

What had tipped her off? And not only did she know, but she was finding it amusing.

"What makes you think Peter getting married is bothering me?" I tried.

She laughed. "Okay, fine," she said. "Whenever you're ready." She seemed to have finished speaking, but she kept looking at me. Finally, she couldn't hold it in any longer. "He'll still be your friend. You guys have known one another since high school."

"He'll be mowing the damn lawn!" I blurted out. "And going to his kids' soccer games, and feeding shrubs, and… and he'll probably someday end up being responsible!"

Nicole laughed harder still. "You've always complained that he was sophomoric," she reminded me.

I considered what she'd said. "I'm going to miss the stupid bastard," I said before laughing some myself.

"So what do you make of 'The doctor is dead'?" I asked.

Nicole sat with both hands wrapped around her cup of tea. She didn't have to ponder before answering. "I think Mrs. Bradley is the type of person who craves attention more than most," she said.

"So it was for the shock value," I more stated than asked. "Like everything else she says, it was meant to make an impression."

"Exactly. Or…" Nicole squinted a bit and held the thought.

"Or she was rejoicing that her husband was gone," I speculated.

Nicole's eyebrows arched as she slowly nodded her agreement.

"Those are the same two possibilities that I arrived at too," I said.

"Yeah, sure," she came back.

"Enough frivolity," I said, getting up. "I've got to get to work."

"You're actually going to pursue this?" she asked. But she didn't really seem all that surprised.

"I feel a tad responsible," I explained. "I at least have to get in touch with Brian. I owe him some sort of an apology. And I've still got Dr. Bradley's check."

Nicole waited. She knew there was more.

"Besides," I said, "you know it's not like in the movies. The police are almost always anxious to close out a case. If it looks like some sort of accident, it'll most likely be ruled an accident."

With the one notable exception that had taken place back when Nicole and I first met, I'd spent the past eighteen months chasing down cheating spouses and deadbeat dads. But my quick-witted Ms. Doucette had her limits and she was kind enough not to remind me of that fact. "Go get 'em, Dean Cello," she offered.

And with that, Nicole went upstairs and left me to my work. Since the Maine timber industry project had taken her through the weekend, she was going to have the next couple of days off. After that, she'd be filling in for Dan, one of the regular co-anchors, doing the evening edition of the News of New England for the remainder of the week.

An online check revealed that the name of the Lynnfield town newspaper was *The Villager*. I called and was told that it was published on Wednesday afternoons for distribution on Thursdays.

After pouring a second cup of coffee, I opened the *Globe* to the obituaries. "Dr. Connor M. Bradley, 59, beloved husband of Ellen Bradley, father of Kevin and Timothy…" Wake tonight, funeral tomorrow.

I went back to the front of the paper and began turning pages one at a time. There just might be a small blurb about a suburban doctor's accidental death. Two-thirds of the way down on page 5, I found it:

> "LYNNFIELD DOCTOR DROWNS IN HOME – Shortly after 9:00 p.m. on Saturday, police were called to the Lynnfield home of 59-year old Dr. Connor Bradley on Thistle Lane. Dr. Bradley's wife Ellen had

returned home to find him laying face down at the bottom of their indoor swimming pool. The State Medical Examiner's office has determined the cause of death to be drowning. Police have ruled the incident an accident."

I went to the phone and called Saint Joseph's Academy in Danvers. A seemingly middle-aged female voice identified the school in business-like fashion.

"Hi. I'm sorry to trouble you, but do you have a number at which I can reach Brian Bradley?"

"Well, I do have his number, but I've been trying unsuccessfully to reach him myself this morning. May I ask who's calling?"

"Of course. I'm his Uncle Michael. Is there a message you want to give Brian should I succeed in tracking him down?"

"No," she replied hesitantly, "We were just wondering where he is this morning."

"Oh, so he didn't call to report that he wouldn't be in today. Well, under the circumstances…"

"The circumstances?" She hadn't heard.

I explained that Brian's uncle, Dr. Connor Bradley, had passed away. The woman at the other end offered her sympathy and asked me to tell Brian that he needn't be concerned about having forgotten to call the school. She gave me the number and wished me good luck.

The number I had; the luck I didn't. Brian's cell was turned off.

With some apprehension, I called Dr. Bradley's house. There was an excellent chance that Brian would be over there.

The Mrs. sounded as composed as ever. "Bradley residence."

"Hi. I'm terribly sorry to be bothering you, but may I please speak to Brian for a moment?"

"Well I suppose you may if you can find him," she replied.

"Ah, so he's not there then."

"Well nobody seems to have any idea *where* he is. Mr. Cello is it?"

"Yes. Again, I do apologize for bothering—"

"Mr. Cello, at the present time, this family has more to be concerned about than a lost dog. Good day." Click.

After checking the atlas, I climbed into the Z4 and drove up to the Brookstone Village condos on Locust Street in Danvers. The place appeared to be rather upscale for someone living on a first year teacher's salary—eight taupe-stained clapboarded buildings staggered on nicely landscaped grounds. The azaleas were in bloom and the aroma of recently spread cedar mulch wafted through the air. A small white sign directed me to the office.

The young woman at the desk was early twenties, rather chunky. She had a pleasant smile. "May I help you?"

"Hopefully," I replied cheerfully. "I'm looking for Brian Bradley. He gave me the number, but I didn't write it down and…" I tapped myself on the side of the head.

"Three-O-six," she replied, without having to look it up. "Have a nice day."

I moved the car over to Building 3.

The directory in the vestibule confirmed that Brian Bradley did indeed live in Unit 306. I rang the bell, waited, rang again, and waited again. Satisfied that nobody was going to respond, I took the elevator up and exited onto beige carpeting. 301 – 306, the arrow pointed to the right. Tract lighting, not too bright. I knocked on the door.

The dog's thunderous bark took me by surprise. I waited for a human voice, but none came. The dog emitted one more, less hardy bark, and then whimpered.

A glance down the hall confirmed that there was nobody else around. I took out my little set of specialty tools. While

I was still asking myself if I really wanted to do this, the tumblers aligned and I found myself pushing the door open a couple of inches. I let the dog sniff my hand through a crack too narrow for him to do any damage, and then when I didn't hear a growl, I opened the door a little more.

A light from the living room revealed that my new acquaintance was a handsomely groomed Airedale, undoubtedly Sir Cedric of Winchester. Sir Cedric seemed to be anything but dangerous. Although he was well mannered enough to remain on all fours, he wagged his tail excitedly and lapped at my hand. When I closed the door behind me and took a step inside, I understood why he was so happy to see me. The stench of dog urine and feces hit me from the far corner of the room. Obviously, Sir Cedric had been alone for a long time.

I called Brian's name, not really expecting to get a response. Then, using my shirttail to touch the switches, I slowly walked through each of the rooms, turning lights on and off as I went. My heart was pounding; I didn't want to find what I feared I might. Behind the shower curtain. Under the bed.

At last, I breathed a heavy sigh of relief. If Brian Bradley had joined his uncle in the great beyond, he hadn't begun the journey from his condo unit. Or at least there didn't seem to be any evidence lending itself to that hypothesis.

But now what? If Brian had indeed been a victim of foul play, I couldn't call the police and announce that I'd just broken in to his home. But I also couldn't bring myself to just leave the poor dog here all by himself. Of course I could place an anonymous call from a pay phone.

I thought about the chunky girl who'd just told me where Brian lived. Nothing I could do about that now.

Sir Cedric sat down, looked at me soulfully and tilted his head to one side.

I never had a dog. As a boy, I'd always wanted one, but

my parents had maintained that the North End was no place for a dog.

Still looking at me, Sir Cedric tilted his head to the other side.

Wasn't this what I was originally hired for after all?

The leash was on a small table by the door where I'd come in.

"Come on, boy. We're going for a ride."

Five minutes later I was motoring down Route 1 with an Airedale sitting in the shotgun seat, hanging his head out the window. I looked over at him and considered the irony. I'd found the dog. And lost both clients.

Chapter 5

I stopped at a convenience store to pick up a couple of cans of dog food and a box of Milk-Bones, then headed straight home. As soon as I got in, I called Nicole on her cell. "Where are you?"

"I'm home. I went out to do the grocery shopping, but I'm back now."

"Come downstairs. There's someone here I want you to meet."

She gave me a tentative "Okay" and said she'd be right down.

A couple of minutes later, Nicole was in my study saying, "Oh, my God, you didn't." But a moment after that, she was on her knees laughing and trying not too hard to keep Sir Cedric from licking her face.

"After I feed my dog, I'm going to take him for a walk up Commonwealth Avenue," I said. "He's a champion, you know."

It was all too obvious that I was making light of having the dog so as to seemingly lessen the seriousness of the situation. Nicole's expression revealed that she was torn between my questionable decision and Sir Cedric's undeniable appeal. I explained how I inadvertently found him and how I couldn't just leave him there with no one to care for him. I further explained that I planned to keep him only until I learned the whereabouts of Brian Bradley.

After listening to my explanation, Nicole said, "I've got a few calls to make. I'll see you when I come to bail you out."

As planned, I took Cedric, I decided to drop the Sir, for a walk up the grass median in the middle of Commonwealth Avenue. There was no doubt in my mind that he was the best-looking, best-behaved dog in the city. I was even beginning to convince myself that other dogs were somehow aware of his championship status. I could have sworn I saw a cocker spaniel and then a golden retriever move out of the way as we approached. A pair of poodles looked up at him in awe. It wasn't until I spotted an oncoming rottweiler that I decided to cross over onto the sidewalk. I didn't want the rottweiler to be embarrassed if Cedric decided to kick his ass.

After dinner that night, Nicole lightened up and joined us as we took a stroll through the Common. I continued to joke about "my dog" and his greatness. Nicole shook her head but obviously didn't totally disapprove.

I figured I wouldn't be able to do any work on the Bradley matter until after the funeral—Wednesday at the earliest. Since Nicole had Tuesday off anyway, we made the most it. We took her Corolla up the coast, Cedric in the back seat with his head outside catching the breeze most of the way. A couple of times he licked Nicole's ear, which made her giggle like a schoolgirl before turning to scratch his neck. In Ipswich, we stopped at Crane's Beach and got out to play for a while. Cedric chased the ball across rolling sand dunes and returned with it every time, but he didn't seem to understand that he had to let go once he'd retrieved it. We'd have to work on that one before taking it to the Common.

At breakfast on Wednesday morning, Nicole, decidedly more serious, revisited a conversation we'd briefly touched upon the day before in the car. "What if Brian Bradley has been murdered?" she asked quite bluntly. "I know you said you were careful in the condo, but the police might still find something. And here you are with the dog. You know I've enjoyed having him too, but…"

I sighed. I wasn't going to get away with anything less than a totally straight answer. "The fact of the matter is I got the distinct impression that Ellen Bradley wasn't particularly fond of Cedric. In fact, the only two people who I'm sure cared about him are in one way or another gone, at least for now. I can't just turn him over to an uncertain fate."

Nicole did her best to show disapproval, but finally gave up. "How can I not love a guy who feels such compassion for animals?"

I also shared with Nicole my belief that the doctor's check might prove useful should I be caught in possession of the dog. It would serve to lend credence to my assertion that I'd been retained to find him—an assertion that Ellen Bradley too could begrudgingly corroborate.

"Speaking of that check," Nicole said, "wouldn't it seem logical that Ellen Bradley has already placed a stop payment on it?"

"I've thought about that," I said. "My suspicion is that she hasn't. In fact, under the circumstances, I doubt that anything dog related has even crossed her mind. Either way, though, it could still prove useful."

Nicole studied me for a moment, and then, with raised eyebrows, nodded her tentative understanding. She wasn't sold, but she also knew that she wasn't going to dissuade me. She got up and gave me a quick good-by kiss before heading upstairs, leaving Cedric and me to sort it all out.

I enjoyed a second cup of coffee while planning my attack, Cedric lying at my feet on the floor of the study. So far all I had to work with were the home addresses and work locations of each of the members of the Bradley clan—not a lot to go on. I'd already called Kevin's office to make a doctor's appointment; the soonest I could get was two weeks from Thursday. After weighing the few available options, I decided the easiest place to start would be Carol Bradley's bookstore.

I knew that the police would conduct a cursory investigation, if for no other reason than to make it appear that they were doing their job. After that, if they thought they might be onto something, they would go back and question certain individuals in greater detail.

Since the family would already have been subjected to the initial questioning, and since nobody was legally obligated to talk to me, I thought it would be best to go incognito. Seeing as it was still early, though, I figured I had time for the sports page before heading out.

I'd been reading for less than a minute when the phone rang. The voice at the other end was that of a male who sounded too polite to be sincere. "Mr. Cello, this is Lieutenant Schmidlin of the State Police. I wonder, sir, if you could pay us a visit this morning at the Peabody barracks?"

Something told me it wasn't really a question. I responded all up beat and innocent. "Certainly, Lieutenant. What time would you like to see me?"

"The sooner the better, sir."

"Then I'll head up right now. May I ask what this is about, though?"

"When you get here, sir."

I didn't bother to call Nicole. She was a girlfriend, not a wife. Why should I be subjected to an I-told-you-so?

Along Storrow Drive, over the Mystic River Bridge, and up Route 1, I drove semi-consciously, thinking of nothing but what the police wanted to talk to me about. The *State* Police. It wasn't likely that dognapping was in their repertoire.

Probably because I was doing so much thinking, I seemed to get there in no time at all. I parked the car off to the side and started toward the double glass doors of the two-story cement block building. *Be casual. Appear relaxed.*

The young, dark-haired trooper at the front desk was on the phone when I walked in. I strolled up and did my best to look nonchalant while waiting for him to finish his conversation—

"That's right, ma'am... You're welcome."

The trooper put down the phone and, stone faced,

directed his attention toward me. "Yes, sir. What can I do for you?"

"Good morning. Dean Cello," I announced with my best casual smile. "I'm here to see Lieutenant Schmidlin."

"First door on the right, sir." He motioned with his thumb over his shoulder and then directed his attention to some papers on the desk in front of him.

Looking over to where he'd pointed, I saw that the first door on the right led to an office that had large glass windows on the two facing sides. The man who I assumed to be my host looked early forties, tall, blonde, and dressed in a charcoal suit, white shirt, and repp tie. He spotted me approaching and opened the door.

"Mr. Cello?" he asked while smiling affably.

"Good morning, Lieutenant." I confirmed my identity with a quick nod and shook his hand. His grip was firm, but not overbearing.

"Thank you for coming," he said as he motioned for me to sit down in the club chair beside his desk. "May I call you Dean?"

"I'd actually prefer that," I told him as I accepted his invitation to sit.

"Good," he said, still smiling agreeably. "As a private investigator, I'm sure you're familiar with police procedure, so I'm hoping we can cut through all the formality and just talk as one professional to another. And please… call me Bob."

"Sounds good to me, Bob," I came back, trying to sound upbeat and casual.

Bob positioned himself behind the desk, leaned back in his swivel chair and clasped his hands together. "So have you found Brian Bradley yet?"

Had my best friend not been a cop, the sudden question might have elicited the response Bob was hoping for. As it was, though, I was familiar with the technique—put the suspect at ease, then surprise him with the sudden bomb.

"Ah," I said casually. "I'm sure you can appreciate that I've been wondering what it was you wanted to speak to me about."

Bob's smile seemed to become a little more plastic than it had been a moment ago. He waited for me to answer the question.

"I'm no longer looking," I told him, maintaining my casual air. "In fact my search, if you can call it that, merely consisted of a couple of unanswered phone calls and a strike-out visit to his condo." I hadn't forgotten the chunky young woman at the Brookstone Village office. "It wasn't that important so I just gave it up."

"But it was important enough that you called the school looking for him." He left the question implied.

"Well, not really," I heard myself say. "Well, I mean, I called the school looking for him, but it wasn't really that important."

Bob's smile seemed to become a bit more menacing. His steel blue eyes remained fixed on mine and it occurred to me that when he wore the state trooper's uniform he must have looked like a Nazi poster boy.

"You know, Bob," I started, "if it's okay with you, I'd just as soon lay the whole Brian Bradley thing out chronologically for you. That way, we'll be sure I don't miss anything." I threw in a minor chuckle for effect. "And it'll save you a lot of questions."

Bob nodded sardonically and waited.

I started all the way back with Dr. Bradley's phone call and went up through to "The doctor is dead." Whatever the Lieutenant was thinking, he didn't let it show.

"So naturally I felt I owed the kid an apology of sorts," I said. "I mean, not that I assumed his uncle had in fact been murdered, but I *had* dismissed the idea rather summarily and I felt badly about that. And I also wanted to express my sympathy."

I paused long enough to force Bob to ask another question. “So after Mrs. Bradley told you the doctor had died, how long did you wait before trying to contact Brian?”

“I tried right away, but his number was unlisted. Or maybe he doesn’t have a landline. Anyway, I forgot about it till the next morning, when I figured I might as well give the school a shot.” On the way over, I’d considered that if the Lieutenant wanted me for questioning concerning Brian Bradley, he’d probably already queried the woman at the school about incoming calls and subsequently learned that “Uncle Michael” had placed his from Dean Cello’s home.

“Why did you identify yourself as an Uncle Michael?”

“‘Hi, you don’t know me; can I have Brian Bradley’s phone number?’ I didn’t think that would have worked too well.”

The lieutenant waited again, the steel blue eyes not blinking.

I continued. “So when he didn’t answer, I figured there was an excellent chance that, with his uncle having passed away, he might be at the doctor’s house with the rest of the family. I then called there and was told that he wasn’t, and that they too didn’t know where he was. Needless to say, I found that odd, so having nothing better to do on Monday morning, I decided I’d take a ride up to his condo and ring the bell. When there was no answer, I turned to leave, but then figured, since I was already there, I might as well go up and knock. So I did. Still nothing. At that point I still thought the whole thing was strange, but for that matter so was being hired to find a dog that wasn’t lost…” I again threw in a minor chuckle. “So I filed it away as slightly interesting, but none of my concern, and went home. That’s it.”

The lieutenant waited for more. This time he didn’t get it.

“Have you found the dog, Mr. Cello?”

What happened to Dean? “I was no longer thinking about the dog, Lieutenant. I suppose that when I received Brian’s phone message on Saturday night, I probably then assumed the dog had been returned to the doctor's home. As I say, though, I was actually no longer thinking about the dog. It hadn't even been lost after all."

"And of course you've returned the doctor's retainer to Mrs. Bradley."

My eyebrows shot up. "You know, now that you mention it, I must do that. I think it's still sitting on my desk."

Again the lieutenant's eyes remained fixed on mine.

I decided it was time to take the initiative. Carefully. "Lieutenant… may I ask… Is Brian Bradley still missing?"

He considered his response before answering. "We're working on it, Mr. Cello. Nobody else needs to be."

I casually nodded my understanding. "And, if I may… naturally, I'm curious… the doctor's death?"

The lieutenant leaned forward in his chair and interlaced his fingers on the desk in front of him. "You were a schoolteacher," he started slowly and with what I took to be some condescension. "High school science. Andover. Nice town. Then you gave it up to do amateur photography." The lieutenant grinned derisively before continuing. "Most of your subjects were married men and their paramours. Then last September you got lucky and cracked a murder case up in Vermont." He paused and smiled knowingly before continuing. "I'm a cop, Mr. Cello. I know what it feels like to solve a case. It's euphoric. It can be addictive if you let it. Don't let it, Mr. Cello. Am I clear?"

"Lieutenant… Bob, for starters, chasing down cheating spouses is tough work, but somebody's got to do it." I laughed as agreeably as I knew how before continuing. "I'm going to be totally honest with you, though. What I like best is not having to set an alarm clock and not having to punch a time clock, even figuratively, and not having to answer to superiors." I softened my expression even more and looked him eye to eye as I delivered the coup de grace. "Bob, if I wanted to be a police officer, I would be."

The lieutenant reverted back to his Bob persona. Coming to his feet, he cuffed me lightly on the arm and headed over to open the door. While I was shaking the hand he'd extended, he said, "I hope you meant what you said, Dean. These matters are best left to the proper authorities. We've got the resources to do the job correctly. And we certainly don't need anybody else around *impeding an official investigation.*" After having slowly articulated those last four words, the lieutenant once again paused for effect. "But I know that you're a man of your word," he resumed. "Hell, I know everything there is to know about you." He flashed an insincere smile. "Isn't technology wonderful?"

Apparently it doesn't know where a certain Airedale is.

I did my best to assure Lieutenant Schmidlin that I had no interest in pursuing either the doctor's death or the nephew's disappearance, if in fact the latter was still an issue. I furthered that I was looking forward to enjoying the summer by taking my early morning runs along the Charles, reading the paper over a cup of coffee, pulling for the Sox, spending a few weekends on the Cape, and taking the occasional picture of a wayward husband when personal finances required that I do so. Boredom wasn't a number that was in my repertoire. Indeed, I fully intended to enjoy up to Labor Day and beyond, free of needless distractions.

The Lieutenant offered yet another insincere smile as he opened the door for me.

Once back in the Z4, I headed east on Route 129 toward Salem. I had a bookstore to browse through.

Chapter 6

I approached the center of the historic coastal city by way of Essex Street. There's something about Salem that has always intrigued me. The old colonial houses set close to the brick sidewalks, the faux-gas streetlights in the center of town—it possesses a certain charm. Along the main streets, many of the old, mostly brown-stained houses, either clapboarded or cedar-shingled, seem to be incongruously interspersed with such small businesses as the Witch City Dairy Barn, the Witch City House of Pizza, and Witch City Foreign Auto. Somebody arriving for the first time might get the idea that the locals were proud of the fact that their forefathers slaughtered nineteen innocent people in a fanatical fit of misguided religious zeal. But of course that organized carnage has become an almost tangible part of the city's history and indeed Salem would not now be Salem without it. At any rate, a visitor to Salem can *feel* history.

I motored through the center and then turned right onto Washington Street. Less than a full block down, again on the right, I spotted the Old Corner Book Store—seemingly an odd name for a place in the middle of the block. Maybe it had moved. The building was actually a two-story house—weathered cedar shingles, pitched roof. The privet hedges were in desperate need of a pruning; they hung out over the grayed picket fence and into the sidewalk area.

A hand-printed sign taped to the oval glass in the front door requested that visitors enter "downstairs." I descended the six brick steps and walked through the already opened door. A single chime resonated melodically as I did so.

Behind a counter to the left of the entrance was a thin young woman who I assumed to be in her late teens—possibly a student at Salem State. I offered her a "Good Morning," and she returned my greeting verbatim, albeit not enthusiastically.

Strolling past her and into the store, I spotted a wooden staircase along the wall to the left. At the base of the stairs stood a metal post atop of which sat a small white sign that read "FICTION." Presumably then, the non-fiction was on the lower level. As I started up the stairs, I noticed that the lighting in the place was perhaps a bit dimmer than might typically be expected.

The upstairs looked pretty much like the downstairs except that there was no desk at the front. A casual stroll through the stacks revealed that there was nobody working on that level. In fact there weren't any customers on that level either.

I went back downstairs and resumed my casual stroll, this time spotting three customers, but still no other employees. Either the doctor's son Kevin had robbed the cradle or his wife Carol was taking the rest of the week off to remain with her husband and mother-in-law.

I returned to the counter. "Excuse me," I said. "I've never been in here before and I've just got to tell you, I really like the feel of this place. Are you the owner?"

The thin girl lifted her eyes up from whatever it was she was reading and looked at me like I was stupid. "I just work here," she said.

"Yeah," I said with a chuckle, "I guess when you're the owner you don't have to work, huh?"

"She *better* be working," came the quick reply. "I've got a class at four."

I smiled agreeably as I started for the door. "Unfortunately, I haven't got time to look around right now. What time does the store close?"

"Six," she said, while looking back down at what I could now see were notes.

"Have a nice day," I told her.

"Yeah, you too," she said without looking up.

Seeing as I was already halfway up the coast, I thought I'd continue on up to Rockport. That was where Jill, Dr. Bradley's other daughter-in-law, had an art gallery. Odds were she too would probably have remained home with the rest of the family, but one never knows. Besides, what else did an unemployed schoolteacher have to do on a Wednesday morning?

I motored up 1A and 127 through Gloucester and into Rockport. The little side street was located about two blocks from the ocean, and immediately after turning onto it, I spied the Perrin Art Gallery—a small, white-clapboarded building on the left. It shared a small parking lot with an antique dealer. I turned in and parked toward the back on the antique dealer's side.

The salty air was invigorating. I took a moment to fill my lungs with it just before passing through the open door.

A dark-haired slender woman of average height, her back to the door, was telling a retired-aged couple how to get to Plum Island. When the couple thanked her and started to leave, she turned to notice me and gave a surprised but subdued, "Hi." I thought her to be in her late twenties. Although not unpleasant to look at, she presented a somewhat austere appearance. Her straight hair, jeans and sweatshirt, and bare minimum of makeup caused me to think her to be rather bohemian.

"Good morning," I offered as pleasantly as I knew how. "Are you the artist?"

"All mine," she said with no hint of pride as she started to walk passed me.

I nodded my acknowledgement and began to browse. All the works on display were seascapes done in the obligatory oils. While pretending to be examining the waves and rocks and lighthouses and sailing ships, I pondered how I was going to initiate a conversation with a person so seemingly detached. I noticed through the corner of my eye that she'd quietly seated herself on a chair by the door through which I'd entered. A few moments later, another glance revealed that she was reading a paperback.

Eventually, my tour around the room having been completed, I had to give it a shot. "I like your work," I said.

She looked up from her book. "It's a living," she came back.

"I'm sure it's more than that," I said, hoping to engage her.

She looked at me for a moment. "You're right, it is," she said. "Sometimes I just come in and paint for the sake of painting."

I don't know what my expression said, but she seemed to feel the need to defend herself. "It's certainly not expressionism or surrealism," she added. "What you see is what you get here."

"I much prefer this to a dripping clock," I told her.

The corners of her mouth turned up into just short of what could legitimately be classified as a smile. She closed her book. "You don't like Dali?"

"Whose he?"

Finally, she did smile some, but with her mouth only; the dark eyes remained solemn.

I tried to maintain what little momentum I had. "If you don't mind me saying so, you sound almost ashamed of the fact that you paint seascapes. What's more beautiful than nature?"

She studied me a moment before responding. "It's not at all a matter of shame," she said. "I love the sea and I love to paint it. What I *don't* like is some avant-garde bore thinking my work is meaningless simply because it makes perfect sense to the conscious mind."

Trying to lighten it up, I offered, "I hope I didn't come across as an avant-garde bore. I really do like your paintings, and…"

"Oh, I didn't mean you," she said, hastening to resolve the apparent misperception. "I just meant…"

"It's okay," I assured her. "I understand."

The ice having been broken, I had a confession of sorts to make. "I truly do like your paintings, but to be honest, I'm not in the market right now. I just happen to be visiting around here. Actually, not under the most pleasant of circumstances I'm afraid."

"Oh?" she queried politely.

"My older sister had an accident—a fatal one as it turns out."

"How terrible," she replied dispassionately.

"Mm. It's not the way one generally expects the end to come, you know? I mean, one day she's there, no illness or anything, then… " I shook my head.

She studied me for a moment. "Funny, I didn't see anything in the paper about it," she said.

"Well it isn't like she's anybody famous," I said. "Besides, she lives… lived… in Wenham. My brother's making the funeral arrangements and all, and I had nothing to do so I thought I'd take a ride up the coast here."

I could see the wheels turning as her eyes remained fixed on mine. "Well if you decide to buy a painting before you leave, you know where to find us," she said. And with that she reopened her book, effectively dismissing me and my sister and her terrible accident. She didn't ask where I was from. She didn't ask what I did for a living. She certainly didn't inquire about the nature of the accident.

I told her I might just do that—come back and buy one of her paintings. We both knew that I wouldn't.

Instead of heading straight toward the car, I crossed the lot and walked into the antique shop. The dealer was a bald, pot-bellied guy pushing sixty.

"Do you happen to have a Sorrento tea cart?" I asked him.

He laughed. "You'd have to get pretty damn lucky to just walk in somewhere and find one of those," he said.

I nodded. "How much are they worth, anyway?"

"Good condition? Somewhere upwards of three thousand."

Three thousand was a drop in the bucket for the Bradley's, but it was still beyond me why anyone would want to spend it on a used piece of furniture. A teacart, no less. But to each his own.

"Hey, can I ask you something?" I said.

"Shoot."

"I was just across the lot in the art gallery. Is it me or is she… unfriendly?"

He looked amused. "She's been over there for three years now. I talked to her once. That was it."

"Can't be good for business."

He shrugged. At his age, he'd given up trying to figure people out.

As I emerged from the antique place and turned to cross the little parking lot, I saw Jill Bradley leaning against the front of her building, arms folded across her chest. She continued to stare straight at me; it was I who finally looked away. While exiting the parking lot, I glanced over to see that she still had not taken her eyes off me. I gave her a friendly little wave and drove back up the street.

The fisherman's platter at Captain Jack's on 127 in Gloucester was outstanding. And it was late enough in the day that it would serve as both lunch and dinner.

Not being in any particular hurry, I took my time winding down secondary roads on the way back south. Here and there I sang along some with Eric Clapton—the *Unplugged* one.

It was almost five o'clock when I again turned onto Washington Street in Salem. I drove passed the bookstore, found a space three or four buildings up, and walked back.

This time the woman behind the counter near the door was a very attractive, thirtyish blonde in a pale blue sweater and off-white chinos. She looked up immediately and acknowledged me with a pleasant smile and a simple but seemingly heartfelt, "Hi."

I returned the greeting and nonchalantly began to browse, but I sensed that her eyes were still on me. A glance in her direction revealed that I wasn't becoming paranoid.

She didn't try to hide the fact that she'd been looking at me. Instead, she displayed that smile again and allowed her eyes to remain fixed on mine. The light from a small lamp on the shelf behind her reflected off her wavy blond hair.

I returned a casual smile as I strolled toward her. "I've never been in here before. Do you specialize in anything in particular?"

"Everything from astrophysics to Zen," she said, the smile becoming broader still.

She'd obviously used the line a thousand times, but I heard myself laughing anyway. "I'm afraid I'm not feeling quite that erudite today," I said as I reached the counter. The close range observation revealed eyes that were pools of emerald green. She was even more attractive than I'd originally thought.

"We can do mundane," she came back. "Even the most erudite individuals need to take a break now and then." She rested her crossed forearms on the counter and leaned toward me. "Anything in particular I can help you with?"

"Well in the wake of astrophysics, I'm sure I'm going to embarrass myself now, but…"

"We don't really sell too many of those," she confessed.

"Well the fact is I'm planning on buying a dog," I told her, "and I'm not sure which breed to select. Do you have anything to offer that's that… mundane?"

She came out from around the counter and silently led me off to the right and down toward the back.

When we arrived at our destination, she crouched down and examined the second shelf up from the floor before placing an index finger on top of one of the bindings. "Do you live alone?" she asked while still looking at the books.

The question took me by surprise and I hesitated for a moment before answering. "As a matter of fact I do. Why?"

She seemed to suddenly realize how off-the-wall her question must have sounded and she started laughing. "I'm sorry," she offered as she looked up and moved a lock of blond hair away from her eye. "I just meant… well I was just trying to figure out what kind of a dog would be right for you."

"Great," I said. "I won't have to buy the book."

She laughed again, even harder this time. "That's not fair," she said. "If I don't sell books, I'll starve."

"Do you live alone?" I asked.

"Oh-ho!" she exclaimed approvingly as she came to her feet with a book in hand. She held it out for my taking.

I took the book from her without looking at it, keeping my eyes focused on her instead. "I tell you what," I said. "Since you're a self-proclaimed expert, let's see if you can figure out what type of dog you think would be right for me, and if I end up taking your advise, I'll buy the book anyway. Just so you won't… you know… starve."

Just then the door chime sounded. "Golden retriever," she said, as she passed by me *en route* to the front of the store.

I glanced at the cover—profiles of a couple of dozen dog breeds on a plain white background.

I followed her, book in hand. "Okay," I murmured tentatively. "But what are you basing that on?"

She didn't answer.

When we got to the front, there was no other customer in sight. If anyone had come in, he or she must have disappeared down one of the other rows of books.

The blonde woman who I assumed to be Carol Bradley silently slid back behind her counter, but when she turned to face me, I saw that she was still wearing a small closed-mouthed smile. Actually, I could probably better describe it as a mischievous grin. She held it as she looked back at me without speaking.

"Why golden retriever?" I asked again.

After studying me a moment longer, she said, "You just look like a golden retriever kind of guy."

I looked away and laughed a bit before looking back at her.

"What?" she demanded playfully.

"Do you base all your perceptions on appearances alone?" I asked.

"Not entirely," she said, cocking her head some. "But I think we all know that appearances do reveal a lot. The style of clothes a person wears, the manner in which he or she speaks, the eye contact—all those things make a statement."

I placed the book down, folded my hands, and leaned on the counter. "Pardon me if I seem a bit self-absorbed here, but you've peaked my curiosity," I said. "So what kind of a guy *is* a golden retriever owner?" Before she could answer, I added, "I mean if I'm projecting the wrong image, I might want to buy a different shirt."

That won me another closed-mouthed smile while she formulated her answer. After some contemplation, she nodded gently and offered, "Kind... intelligent... a quiet confidence..."

"Totally wrong," I told her. "I'm nasty, stupid, and socially inept."

Her eyes widened and she laughed again. "And a liar," she said. "You're a liar. Although a horrible one."

"Dave," I professed as I offered my hand across the counter.

"Carol," she said, as she squeezed—no shake, just a squeeze.

"You know, it occurs to me, Carol, that you'd be much more capable of determining which breed of dog would suite me best if you knew me better. May I take you to dinner tonight?"

Before she even spoke, her expression said I was about to get shot down. "Oh, I'm afraid I really can't tonight," she said. But then her eyebrows arched. "But if tomorrow night would be okay…"

"Tomorrow night would be perfect," I assured her.

That closed-mouthed smile was most definitely mischievous now. The temperature in the bookstore was ten degrees warmer than when I'd walked in.

"Why don't you meet me at Olivia's?" she almost whispered.

Since we had no acquaintances in common that she was aware of, I assumed Olivia's to be a restaurant. The phone book would answer the related questions.

"How's six-thirty?" I asked.

"Six-thirty would be perfect," she said.

I started for the door. "Tomorrow night then."

"I'll look forward to it." The emerald eyes sparkled.

The chime sounded again as I exited.

While driving back toward Boston, I felt a bit guilty about having been so duplicitous with Carol Bradley, but the fact that she was a married woman made it easier for me to rationalize. Imagine her being so blatantly flirtatious. And her husband was a doctor no less.

As I crossed the Tobin Bridge, I considered whether or not I was going to mention my upcoming date to Nicole. Not only did she always express an interest in even my most ordinary cases, but she was also an excellent sounding board and often provided valuable insight as well. The question, of course, was would she get upset about me taking a hot married blonde to dinner?

I remembered once reading that every lie is an act of cowardice, the premise being that the fabricator is in one way or another fearful of the truth. That made sense. I was going to have to face up to it. I was a coward.

Chapter 7

The early edition of the evening news consisted of the usual conglomeration of politics, terrorism, embezzlement, and murder, with the obligatory little feel good piece at the end. As always, Nicole delivered it all impeccably. Back in the early days of our relationship, I had questioned how a woman who professed to empathize to such a degree could serve it all up so casually. Her response was that whatever she related had already happened.

After the news, I updated my notes on what I now considered the Bradley case, and then Cedric and I watched the ballgame. I enjoyed a glass of Chianti and most of a can of hickory smoked almonds; he appeared to enjoy his biscuits. During the top of the fifth inning, we wrestled on the floor with a pull toy Nicole had bought him the day before.

The game was tied at six when Nicole came back on again at ten o'clock, but this dilemma was nothing new. I resurrected a tactic I'd become proficient at just before the last baseball season ended. I simply switched back and forth, focusing on key moments in the ballgame, while being careful to get a glimpse of each of the items Nicole talked about on her newscast. Knowing how women tend to read in things that aren't there, I didn't want her to think I cared more about baseball than I did about some third grader winning the regional Spelling Bee in Skowhegan, Maine.

The Sox won seven to six in the tenth and the news was the same as it had been four hours ago with a fire in Chelsea thrown in.

When Nicole got home, I had a second, smaller, glass of wine, while she enjoyed her first and we chatted for a while in the study. She asked me if I'd made any progress in the Bradley matter and I told her about Lieutenant Schmidlin, my visit with Jill, and my subsequent visit with Carol, minus the date. Why get her nervous for nothing? Besides, she looked great and I was feeling pretty horny.

The next morning, after I'd returned from my run and showered, we were having breakfast when Nicole mentioned that the weatherman was predicting a summer-like day with possible record-breaking temperatures.

"Well we New Englanders are used to that," I casually commented. "You wake up one day and it's summer."

"True," she concurred. "Today's the day the flowers shoot up suddenly, all the birds start singing, and Mozart's…" She squinted a bit and caulked her head. "What's the name of that spring-has-sprung piece?" she asked.

"I know what you mean, but I can't think of it right now either," I told her. I took another bite of my toast.

Nicole was still thinking. "What is the name of that thing?" she repeated, more to herself.

"Forget it," I urged. "I've got my little man working on it."

She looked at me. "Your little man?"

"Mm-hmm."

She waited while I swallowed a piece of toast.

"You know how sometimes you can't remember something, like the title of an old movie or the name of a professor you had in college or… or a piece of music? Well if you just let it go, when the question occurs to you again later, the answer is there too. That's because while you were going about your other business, the little man in your brain was busy going through all the file cabinets until he found it."

"What does he look like?" she wanted to know.

"I picture him a lot like the Monopoly man."

"The little guy with the thick white mustache."

"Right." I took another bite of toast.

Nicole closed her eyes and shook her head, but the upturned corners of her mouth gave her away. "First a stolen dog and now a little man in your brain. I better not leave you alone for four days anymore."

"Crazy like a fox, huh? And he's not stolen. He's in protective custody."

"Whatever he is, I'd better get him outside," she said as she got up from the table. We had decided that it might be a good idea for me not to be seen in the company of an Airedale for a while.

A few minutes after Nicole and Cedric went out the door, I was just about to do the same when the phone rang. It was Peter.

"Hey, pal, I've got the morning off. What are you up to?"

"I've got to go to Lynnfield to buy a newspaper."

"Lynnfield," he repeated. "Must still be the case of the dog that isn't lost."

"That he isn't," I assured him.

"Whatever," he said. "I've got a couple of local errands to do and then you can tell me about it over breakfast."

"How long are your errands going to take?"

"Less than an hour."

I had to head north on Route 1 anyway. I told him I'd see him at his place in an hour.

It was already warm enough to put the top down on the Z4—the first time since last fall. It felt like it did when I cracked the case in Vermont.

Twenty minutes later, I pulled into the parking lot of a White Hen Pantry on Main Street in Lynnfield. I bought a copy of *The Villager* and brought it back out to the car. In the bedroom community's little town paper, the doctor's death was front-page news:

LOCAL DOCTOR DIES IN ACCIDENT

> Dr. Connor Bradley was in his twenty-ninth year of practicing medicine in the town of Lynnfield when tragedy struck this past Saturday night. In keeping with his nightly tradition of going for a swim in his indoor pool, the doctor apparently dove too deep and sustained what turned out to be a fatal injury. Paramedics were called to the scene by his wife Ellen, who returned from the North Shore Mall shortly after 9:00 p.m. and found him lying face down in the water. Although an autopsy revealed that Dr. Bradley had suffered a fractured skull, the official cause of death was determined to be drowning.

The article went on to explain that Connor Bradley had grown up in the affluent suburb of Winchester before receiving his undergraduate degree in biochemistry at Dartmouth. Prior to attending BU Medical, he had taken a year off to perform volunteer work in Guatemala. His wife Ellen was active in several community organizations including the Garden Club and the Friends of the Library. Dr. Kevin Bradley, Connor's son, would be maintaining his father's medical practice in Lynnfield. The younger Dr. Bradley was also the president of the Parents Club at Saint Joseph's Elementary School in Danvers. Timothy, the younger son, owned a pharmacy in the neighboring town of Wakefield, where he also managed the high school baseball team in the spring and coached basketball in the winter.

I placed the paper on the passenger seat and stared up at the clear blue sky. True, these were new bits of information, but the Bradley's all sounded so squeaky clean.

I remembered Brian. I picked up the paper again and went through it page by page. Then I went through it page by page again. There was absolutely nothing in there about his disappearance. Interesting, but not at all helpful.

I headed back south through Saugus and Revere, considering how little I had to work with. Lieutenant Schmidlin, on the other hand, had a wealth of technology at his disposal, not to mention a staff of highly trained professionals. And he would also have access to the patients, which was beginning to look more important than ever.

About twenty minutes after having left Lynnfield, I rolled into the sleepy little seashore community of Winthrop, where Peter lived. The bright sunlight reflected off the ocean to my left and a salty breeze blew at my hair. I would have felt even better if I'd had even an iota of a lead in the Bradley case.

As I pulled up to the humble white cape that Peter and Linda had closed on just a couple of months ago, I spotted my old friend sitting on the brick steps reading the paper. He actually looked like he belonged. When he heard the car stop at the curb, he looked up, then stuffed the paper behind the storm door and headed up the walkway.

"Mind if we take yours?" I called as I turned off the engine and got out.

Peter reached in his pocket for his keys as he turned and cut across the small lawn, heading for his Explorer in the driveway. As he did so, I noticed that the grass had that deep green color and was all nice and even, recently cut.

"When did you get a lawnmower?" I asked.

"Couple of weeks ago," he said as though it were perfectly normal. "Man, after I dethatched, limed, and put down that high nitrogen Turf Builder, it really took off," he added.

Once in the Explorer, I asked Peter if he had ever been in Lou's Donut Shop in Lynnfield. He said he hadn't. I told him how exceptionally good the donuts were and suggested I point the way.

"You're a sadist," he said. "Making a cop eat donuts on his day off."

We rode with the windows open, enjoying what felt like the first day of summer. I filled Peter in on everything that had happened so far in the Bradley affair, including the fact that I had a date with a married woman in less than nine hours.

We were already on Main Street, just a couple of blocks from Lou's, when without warning, Peter suddenly made a left turn down a side street.

"Where are you going?" I asked.

"Linda's back doctor lives down here," he said.

"But you said Linda was in work."

"She is," he said. "I just want to show you where her back doctor lives."

I looked over at him as he continued to drive. "Not for anything, but why would I care where Linda's back doctor lives?"

"You would if you had a bad back," he said.

"But I *don't* have a bad back."

"But you would if you did."

Why fight it? I waited for the house.

A moment later Peter pointed to an oversized yellow garrison with a two-car garage. "There it is," he said.

"Thanks."

When we walked into Lou's, I saw Peter look up at the green zinc ceiling, then down at the worn wooden floor, then over at the pot-bellied stove. "Looks like a place I know up in New Hampshire," he said.

"I'm sure there must be a lot of places that look like this up in New Hampshire," I said. "But only the newer ones."

"Hey, your girlfriend's from the Granite State," he pointed out.

"She couldn't help that," I told him. "She's civilized now."

Once seated with two jelly donuts in front of him, Peter asked, "So other than your date tonight, what's your plan?"

"'The doctor is dead.' I thought I might tail her." I shrugged.

"It's better than anything else you've got so far. But she knows you're Dean Cello, finder of lost dogs. You'll need my car."

"Mm, I thought of that," I said. "Schmidlin too. I'd prefer he not see a midnight blue Z4 tooling around Lynnfield for a while."

Peter lifted a donut but then put it back down again. "You do realize how long the odds are here," he said.

"Yeah, I know," I agreed. "But I figure they improve with each passing day. Time is always of the essence to the police, right? They have other matters to tend to, and resources are usually limited. I doubt that Schmidlin will be able to invest the time I will."

I took Peter's lack of response as tacit agreement. He bit into his jelly donut. "Good donut!" he said.

"Well, you're an authority," I conceded.

"Hey, this was your idea," he pointed out.

"You're right," I said. "Every once in a while." I watched him attack his donut. "How many of those things do you eat in a week, anyway?"

"Not that many," he said. "Just one or two a day."

I didn't say a word, but he must have read something. "No, I shouldn't eat donuts at all," he began, "And I shouldn't smoke, and I shouldn't drink, but what I should do is get up before the friggin' birds every morning and run, not walk, to nowhere until I get back to where I started from. Man, that's living."

He had me smiling, but I refrained from comment.

"Let me ask you something," he continued with an edge. "What's all that exercising going to get you? Another five years? And if you added up all the time you spent exercising, it would probably total what—five years? And was the actual act of exercising any fun? No. So in effect, you extended your life by five years that were all miserable." He took another bite of his donut, this time with a vengeance. "If I get hit by a truck tonight, I won," he said.

The certain knowledge that he was dead serious made it impossible for me to contain my amusement any longer. "You're a sick bastard," I told him.

"Sick my ass," he said before taking a drink of his coffee.

Since I had him on the ropes anyway—"What's with this 'my ass' thing?" I said.

"What are talking about? Why are you talking about your ass?"

"Not *my* ass. *Your* ass."

"*My* ass? Why are you talking about my ass? Keep your distance!"

As always, his anger had dissipated as quickly as it had emerged, but he could never play the straight man for more than a couple of seconds. As soon as the words were out of his mouth he started to laugh—just his normal laugh as opposed to the full-blown spasm that he seemed to reserve for special occasions.

He looked across the table at me as he chewed and swallowed the final bite of his first jelly donut. "You know, I'd tell you to stay out of the way of the State Police…" He lifted his coffee and took another sip, then placed the cup back down on the table. "But I know you wouldn't listen. I remember when we were in high school and you… you tried very hard to make the starting lineup—extra batting practice, Norton hitting you ground balls while the rest of us were leaving…"

"A great athlete I wasn't," I admitted.

"You sucked. But you were as tenacious as a terrier. When you did play, you played as hard as anyone. And that's what you'll do now, no matter what your more sensible old pal tries to get through to you." He almost took a bite out of the second donut, but instead decided to add something else.

"Actually, it's one of the few things I like about you, you miserable schoolteacher."

"Tenacious as a terrier," I paraphrased. "That's a rather creative comparison for an ex-jock cop." I nodded in mock admiration.

"I heard it on TV," he said. "And you can call it what it is. I'm familiar with the term metaphor."

"Well technically, it's not a metaphor. It's a simile."

"Simile my ass." He chomped into the second donut. "So when am I going to meet your dog?" he asked.

"Come to think of it, he's a terrier and he's not all that tenacious."

"Figures. They probably sent him to obedience school at Harvard."

Peter inhaled the last of his second jelly donut just as I was finishing off my single sugared cruller. We sat and chatted over what was left of our coffees. I explained that I planned to conduct my investigation the same way I had originally learned how to use a computer – trial and error, click somewhere and see what happens.

"Actually, I understand that," he said. "Like when you're driving somewhere and you get lost and then you come out to someplace you know and you say, 'Hey, look where I am.'"

"Exactly."

After we emerged from Lou's and were walking toward the Explorer, Peter looked back at the place and nodded his approval. "Great donuts," he conceded. "If I take a heart attack tonight, it was your fault." I didn't bother to remind him that he'd have won.

We drove back to Peter's house where we swapped cars. Seeing the front steps reminded me that he had been waiting when I arrived a while ago.

"You know," I said, "despite your legendary insanity, there is something I have to give you credit for and I don't think I've ever mentioned it before. You're always… *always* punctual."

He looked at me for a moment. "I didn't know it bothered you," he said.

"No. I'm serious on this one."

After getting my sunglasses and my Rex Sox cap out of the Z4's glove compartment, I was walking back over toward the Explorer when a butterfly fluttered across my path. As soon as it did so, I became aware of several singing finches in a nearby maple tree and I simultaneously noticed the half-opened tulips in the flowerbed of the house across the street. *Not Mozart. Vivaldi.* "From *The Four Seasons*!" I rejoiced aloud.

Peter was still standing over by the Explorer. "You okay there, pal?"

"Absolutely." I was still smiling as I tossed him the keys to my car.

"I'm glad you're happy," he said. "You won't mind if I redline it."

"And you won't mind if I burn your new house down."

We nodded our mutual agreement and, donned in baseball cap and shades, I again pointed a vehicle towards Lynnfield.

My first stop was the town library. *The Villager* had said that Mrs. Bradley was a friend of it. It was unlikely that I'd run into Schmidlin in the library, so I took the liberty of removing my disguise before going in.

A heavyset woman wearing a flowered sundress of blue and yellow looked up from the desk and greeted me with a silent smile.

Doing my best to be charming, I offered, "Hi. I just moved into town and I'm trying to familiarize myself. Do we have a town newspaper?"

I hadn't noticed the stack of *Villagers* piled on the left

side of the desk in front of me. The woman in the flowered dress pealed off the top copy and passed it across while giving me a "You're lucky it didn't bite you" look. I thanked her and, paper in hand, seated myself at a round table over by the periodicals.

After spending about fifteen minutes going through the rest of the paper, I returned to the counter, where the woman in the flowered dress was busy scanning returned books. Placing the neatly refolded paper down on the desk, I casually commented, "What a terrible thing about that doctor, huh?"

She stopped scanning and shook her head sympathetically.

"Did you know him?" I asked.

She looked at me and nodded affirmatively before whispering, "His wife is active here at the library. He really was a wonderful man. We'll all miss him."

"What a shame," I commiserated. "And certainly, since you know his wife so well, it's got to be all that more difficult for you."

She half squinted and looked up into her own head for a second before answering. "Actually, we don't see her as much as we used to," she thought out loud. Before I could respond, she gave me a polite, "Excuse me," and then lifted a small pile of books and headed out toward the stacks. Apparently I hadn't been as charming as I had hoped.

On the way out, I stopped to peruse a corkboard that was positioned not far from the door. Posted there were several clipped newspaper photos—local officials with children holding plaques, the girls high school basketball team, and a middle-aged man with his arm around a woman who was beaming. I had to look twice. Indeed the woman in the photo was Ellen Bradley, eyes wide, wearing a broad smile. Unless she had a twin sister, she actually appeared to be capable of being spontaneous. The man gripping her tightly around the shoulders was probably a few years her junior, quite bald, jacket and tie. An attached newspaper article confirmed the fact that the woman in the photo was Ellen Bradley and identified the man as Dr. Harold Golden of Saugus. The pair had just completed the most successful fundraiser in the library's history. March 25 was the dateline on the newspaper.

I remembered Brian saying that when the boulder came down off the Walnut Street overpass, Dr. Bradley had been on his way home from Dr. Golden's house in Saugus. Didn't Saugus have a library?

I exited the library, climbed into the Explorer, and headed out toward Route 1, thinking of nothing but the photo and its possible implications. But certainly Dr. Bradley couldn't have been that naive. Evidently I was reading too much into it, probably because I wanted to. But she looked so… unstiff.

I shook my head and decided I'd come back to it with a clearer perspective later. Right now I had to go home and get ready. I had a date tonight.

Chapter 8

Olivia's was located on Bridge Street, just off the Center. I arrived about five minutes early and discovered that the reservation hadn't been necessary. Despite the fact that it looked like a fine establishment, about a third of the tables were still empty. I presented myself to the maitre d' as Dave Snell and he escorted me to a corner booth, just as I had requested on the phone.

While nursing a glass of cabernet sauvignon, I took in the general ambiance—glass shade-covered candles atop white linen tablecloths, burgundy carpeting, off-white woodwork, very clean—middle-of-the-road comfortable. As I sat there waiting, my imagination took over and I pictured Kevin Bradley storming in demanding to know why I was meeting his wife for dinner. I pictured myself saying, "Wife?! Why, I had no idea." Or maybe I'd just knock him on his ass.

My daydream was brought to an abrupt halt when a striking blonde in a red cotton sweater slid into the seat across the table from me. She had her hair tied up and, although I'd seen her approaching, it wasn't until she sat down across from me that I actually recognized her.

"Been waiting long?" she asked, flashing that winning smile.

"Not at all," I said agreeably. "It's not even twenty of."

"But it would still depend on what time you got here," she pointed out.

I was still trying to come up with something equally clever when she spoke again. "I'm so glad to see you," she said while briefly placing her hand on top of mine. "I had the feeling you weren't going to show up."

"Why would you think that?"

"Just a feeling." She smiled coyly and tossed back her hair. Somehow she didn't strike me as a woman who'd had a lot of experience at being stood up.

"You look great," I heard myself say.

She smiled approvingly.

The waiter appeared and, after introducing himself as Enrique, asked if the lady would like something to drink. Carol looked at my nearly empty glass and then up at me.

"Cab," I told her.

"Excellent," she said. "I'll have the same."

"Why don't you bring us a bottle," I implored Enrique.

After he went on his way, I asked Carol if she'd given any further thought to my dog quandary. "I thought that's why we were here," she reminded me. "I have to get to know you first."

"I'm kind, intelligent, and I project a quiet confidence," I told her.

"That's interesting," she said. "Somebody told me you were nasty, stupid, and socially inept."

"Don't believe him."

Still smiling, Carol asked, "So what's your story, Dave..."

"Snell," I misinformed her. "Why do I have to go first?"

"Because I *asked* first."

"Fair enough," I agreed and launched into the lie I'd prepared on the way over. Since I knew more about teaching than anything else, I usually used that as a cover, but in this instance, I couldn't be sure whether or not Dr. Bradley or his nephew had mentioned anything about Dean Cello to anyone else in the family, so I couldn't get that close. Since Nicole had pretty much familiarized me with how a TV newsroom operates, I figured I'd go with that. I was the person who made the logistical arrangements for the human-interest segments.

"That sounds quite interesting," she said as though she actually meant it.

Enrique returned with our bottle of wine. I simply nodded and he graciously did the honors. As soon as he left, Carol held her wine glass up in such a way that it seemed she actually wanted me to notice the wedding ring.

"So how long have you been married?" I asked quite casually.

With equal nonchalance, she said, "Going on five years."

"And does your husband know you're out to dinner with a kind, intelligent, confident—"

"Specifically, no," she interrupted. "But it's okay. We have an arrangement."

"Interesting," I muttered, but I must have looked like I was thinking something more.

"What?" she asked.

"Call me old fashioned," I said, "but I think that if you were my wife, I wouldn't want to share you."

"That's sweet," she said. She fixed her mouth in that mischievous grin and her emerald eyes seemed to sparkle in the candlelight. I had to remind myself why I was there.

"Your turn, Carol…"

She made me wait a moment while she took a sip of wine.

"Svenson," she proclaimed. I nodded as she cupped her glass in both hands and matter-of-factly took me through her entire life in not much more than two minutes. She had grown up outside of Bloomington, Minnesota, come east to get her BA in English Literature at Wellesley College, married a local guy who had just graduated from Harvard Law, and she now lived with him in Danvers. Indeed, she was well practiced; I almost wondered if I had the right Carol.

When it was my turn to lie again, I contended that I'd grown up in Andover, Mass. and received my communications degree locally at Merrimack College. We talked briefly about our childhoods, real or imagined, and then I tried to steer the conversation in a more useful direction.

"It must be difficult to leave your family behind and relocate the way you did. Are you close to your in-laws?"

"Yes, I am. Well, most of them, anyway."

I offered a casual look of anticipation, but it didn't elicit anything further. Instead, she rested her elbows on the table and, with both hands still wrapped around her glass, she gently swirled her wine while gazing directly into my eyes.

Enrique returned and asked us if we needed a few more minutes before ordering. I thanked him for his graciousness, and after he left, we glanced at the menus and made quick decisions. Carol chose the baked stuffed haddock and I selected the prime rib. She had almost completely drained her glass already; I refilled it.

I couldn't come back to the in-laws too quickly, so I had to settle for perfunctory conversation, which I had to admit was actually rather pleasant. Although I knew that only a portion of what she was proffering was true, she wasn't hard on the eyes. Additionally, knowing that she was lying seemed to somehow enhance her appeal. I think it made her seem even naughtier still. Again I had to remind myself why I was there.

Eventually, as we were nearing the end of the main course, I thought the time might be right to try again. After filling her glass one more time, I asked, "So what's being married like? I mean really?"

She laughed before answering. "I don't know if I'm the right person to ask," she said. "We're not all that conventional."

"No, not just the relationship with the spouse," I explained. "All those extra people that come along with the whole thing. I mean it's not like you want to marry an entire family, and yet there they are—Thanksgiving, Christmas, birthdays, casual visits. I don't know that I could handle it."

"Actually, I rather like my in-laws," she stated quite believably.

"Really," I said, showing measured surprise. "Surely you can't like them *all*."

She emitted a barely audible "Well," before raising her glass to take yet another sip of wine.

"Ah-huh," I pounced playfully.

She started laughing and placed the glass back down on the table. With her other hand she reached over and gripped my forearm. "You're not going to make me be bad," she insisted.

That was an invitation for a line if I'd ever heard one, but I yet again reminded myself which mission I was on and feebly settled for, "I wouldn't think of it."

She gave a single nod so as to indicate that the subject had effectively been concluded.

We looked at one another.

"It's the mother-in-law, isn't it?" I asked.

She started laughing again, harder this time.

"It's always the mother-in-law." I shook my head. "Well now you've peaked my curiosity. I've got to know all about her."

"So you live in Winthrop," she digressed. "What brought you into a bookstore in Salem?"

I probably wouldn't get another chance; I had to go for it. "I'm sorry. It's just that my best friend is getting married in October. I guess it's been making me think about marriage in general lately. I'll be going on thirty-two in June. And I'm an only child." It occurred to me that I was inadvertently being painfully honest.

She placed her hand on mine again and this time she left it there. Her eyes softened as she leaned closer, as if to invite me to talk about it.

I didn't want it to get too heavy. "He's going to have it easy though. His would-be mother-in-law passed away before he even met his fiancée." As an afterthought, I added, "Why is it that husbands and mothers-in-law are usually like oil and water but wives and fathers-in-law get along famously?"

Apparently, she didn't share my desire to keep it light. "You're thirty-two. You must have been in love at some point," she prompted, almost in a whisper.

I was going to have to take the long route. "Mm, a few years ago. But it didn't work out."

She squeezed my hand a bit. "You got hurt," she empathized.

"I survived," I responded cavalierly.

She placed her other hand under mine so that she was now holding my one hand in both of hers. "Tell me about your friend," she said.

Since I hadn't anticipated this subject, I had to play it straight except that I made Peter a teacher—history. I explained how we had been friends since high school and how he had, until recently, retained a sophomoric attitude about everything but his work. I admitted that, despite my having always complained about his lack of maturity, I was now finding his sudden growth unsettling. It wasn't until I actually finished that I realized I had shared my feelings all too honestly. Perhaps it had been a combination of the wine, her warm hands, and those seemingly caring emerald pools. I silently cursed myself. But then something totally unexpected happened.

"I don't really have an arrangement with my husband," she blurted, albeit almost in a whisper. Her eyes softened still more. "The truth is marriage just isn't doing it for me. And recently something happened that made me think about how fleeting life is. So I figured what my husband doesn't know won't hurt him, right?" She seemed to be considering something, and then gave a quick headshake and said, "But you seem like such a nice guy. It wouldn't be fair to get you involved." She suddenly withdrew her hands and began gathering up her handbag.

I reached across the table and gently moved her hand away from the bag. "We're here. It's only dinner. Why don't you tell me about it."

She froze and looked over at me. "I don't want to bore a perfect stranger with my troubles," she said. But her face told a different story.

"Perfect stranger?" I teased. "I just shared my innermost feelings with you. You know how we guys hate that."

That prompted a brave little smile and she placed her bag back down on the seat. "My husband's not a lawyer," she confessed. "He's a doctor." She laughed a bit at the way it came out and then added, "And he didn't go to Harvard; it was Loyola."

"Chicago, I believe?"

She gave a dismissive nod and moved on. "The rest was basically true. I don't know why I lied. I guess I didn't want to take a chance on you somehow figuring out who I was. I suppose that was silly." She closed her eyes and shook her head briefly. Then she looked off to one side and took a deep breath before turning back towards me. When our eyes met again, she smiled more lightheartedly and then took the liberty of pouring herself what was left of the wine.

Over the next half-hour or so, Carol Bradley related to me how she had seemed to lose interest in her marriage over the past ten months or so. She was careful never to mention the names Kevin or Bradley, and I got the impression that everything she was saying was indeed the truth. Obviously, she had needed to talk to someone and, despite her proclamation that she got along well with her in-laws, this understandably wasn't a subject one would typically want to broach with in-laws. And like many other women, she was probably still too embarrassed to share it with friends.

"You mentioned that something had happened recently that made you think about how fleeting life was."

"I can't talk about it yet," she said.

I nodded my understanding.

She reached for my hand again and said, "You *are* a kind, intelligent guy."

I had to force myself to get back to work. Jovially, I offered, "So now that you know you can trust me, you can tell me all about your crazy mother-in-law."

Possibly caught off guard for a moment, she brightened and admitted, "Ah, it's not just her. My sister-in-law's a Grade A weirdo, my…" She thought better of it. But then, looking down at the table and smiling with her mouth only, she confessed, "The truth is the only one I really like a lot is my father-in-law." She said it as though he were still alive, but the sorrow in her voice was evident.

Over coffee, we chatted leisurely and gazed at one another until Carol finally reached over and firmly grasped my hand again. The mischievous grin returned. She leaned in closer again and fixed her eyes on mine. I felt the beast within me stir. We'd stopped talking, but we were doing a lot of breathing. Then, just when I decided not to kiss her, I did. Well actually, she kissed me. But I didn't fight it.

When our lips parted, we looked at one another for a moment before I awkwardly checked my watch and declared that I had to get going. Understandably, Carol looked surprised. "Yeah, it's getting late," she managed.

Out on the sidewalk we'd walked only a short distance before Carol reached her parked car. I told her I'd drop by the bookstore sometime soon. "I still want to buy a dog," I awkwardly joked.

"I'd like that. You stopping by I mean," she said.

By the time I reached my car I was fraught with guilt on two fronts. Although I couldn't deny that this woman was quite attractive, bright, and reasonably pleasant, I knew I wasn't going to risk what I had with Nicole for her. I was merely using her to gain information. It was despicable. And speaking of Nicole, what was I doing cozying up to a married blonde?

Cedric greeted me enthusiastically when I arrived home. I told him he'd have to wait for Nicole to go out, gave him a biscuit, and then sat on the floor with him. The late edition of Nicole's news had just begun, but it occurred to me that I didn't know what was going on in the ballgame. I'd been so preoccupied thinking about Carol and Ellen Bradley that it hadn't occurred to me to turn the radio on in the car.

As usual, I did my switching channels thing so as not to miss any of the game while making sure I still caught enough of the news to make conversation about.

The Sox pulled it out with a sacrifice fly in the bottom of the ninth, a fire ripped through an abandoned warehouse in Quincy, an East Boston man threw his TV set out a third story window because nothing he liked was on, and in Lawrence a thirty-three-year-old man was arrested for the sexual assault of a seventy-one-year-old self-avowed lesbian.

As was our usual habit whenever Nicole came home late, we had a glass of wine and chatted in the study before going off to bed. Cedric assumed his usual position on the bedroom side of the threshold.

The next morning at breakfast, Nicole asked, "So what do you make of that woman in Farmington?"

"Mm," I muttered and went straight for my coffee.

"What do you think could have happened?"

"Who knows?" I chomped into my English muffin. "So today's Friday. You're doing the news tonight and then you're off the weekend, right?"

Nicole looked a bit bewildered. "I thought that was the sort of thing you'd be interested in," she said. "Someone disappearing without a trace like that."

I had to offer something. "I'd imagine that's got to be pretty tough on the family. No closure, you know?"

She looked further perplexed. "There *was* no family.

Unless of course you count the..." She interrupted herself and then asked the question as though she couldn't remember the answer. "How many cats were there?"

"I'm not sure exactly. A few though."

Nicole had stopped eating her Cheerios. "Fifty-two," she informed me. "I'd say that's a few more than a few." Her eyes narrowed. "Didn't you catch my report last night?"

"Of course I did. Wouldn't miss you for anything," I insisted.

Apparently I was less than convincing. She put down her spoon. "You know, Dean," she started, "its okay if you don't watch each and every report I do. I never said I expected you to."

Maybe if I had said something, anything. But I didn't know what to say.

Nicole shook her head, got up, and dumped what was left of her cereal. It was suddenly very quiet. Cedric tucked his tail between his legs and crept over to the far side of the table.

The silence was killing me. "Look," I began, "I saw the warehouse fire, I saw the TV that landed on the neighbor's car, I saw the old lesbian and the thirty-three-year-old pervert—"

"You're missing the point," she interrupted. "You're not obligated. You shouldn't feel as though you have to watch the news just because I'm delivering it." I had never seen her get angry before. She even did *that* with style, not raising her voice despite the fact that she was obviously ticked.

I got up and started toward her.

"What am I upset about, Dean?" she asked.

That I didn't watch you do the news?

"You still don't get it, do you?"

My less than intelligent expression must have confirmed her suspicion.

"Do you think I'm so insecure that I'm going to fall to pieces if you don't watch me do the news?"

I was still considering whether or not the question was rhetorical when she went on to explain. "It isn't that you didn't watch me do the news. That's fine. It's that you think I'll be *upset* if you don't watch me do the news. What am I, some pathetic fragile little…" She thought of something else that apparently was even more important. "And you've been lying. If you'd lie about something like this…" She left the rest implied. She just stood there waiting for me to say the wrong thing. Whatever I said would be the wrong thing.

Eventually, I couldn't take it anymore. I approached her carefully and offered, "Look, Nicole. I never meant to upset you. The truth of the matter is, whenever the ballgame runs late, I switch back and forth so that I won't miss anything that happens in the game and I can still see you do the news at the same time. And I've never actually lied to you. I never said 'I watch the news all the way from beginning to end and I don't watch the ballgame.' I just didn't want to hurt your feelings. It doesn't mean that I consider you a wimp. I just… I just didn't want to hurt your feelings. I love you. You know I love you."

She looked at me for a long time before speaking. Finally, she said, "Tell the little man in your brain to go back three spaces. He won't be getting past Go tonight."

Chapter 9

Oh yeah? Well I had a date with a married woman last night. And man was she hot! "Fine."

Without saying anything further, Nicole picked up Cedric's leash from the kitchen counter and headed for the door. She had returned from their morning walk only a half-hour ago, but apparently she found his company more pleasant than mine. At the sound of the leash jingling, Cedric jumped up excitedly and trotted past me, over to Nicole. I guess I knew where I stood.

Since she was taking "my" dog for a walk, I figured she couldn't be too upset with me. At any rate, she'd get over it. I had to get back to work on the Bradley matter.

The first call I placed was to Peter. "I need you to run one for me."

"Shoot."

"Carol Svenson, Minnesota." I had an afterthought. "And while you're in there, check out Jill Perrin too. Just try Massachusetts." I was going on the possibility that the name of the art gallery was Jill's maiden name. "In fact, you might as well see if you've got anything on Kevin or Timothy Bradley too. And Ellen and Brian. And the doctor, Connor."

"Great. And when you get me fired you can put me on your payroll in charge of the lost dog division."

"It's a deal."

I made the next call and learned that the Garden Club would be meeting on Tuesday at one. Yes, perhaps I would apply for membership, thank you very much.

There were still two more calls I had to make, but they couldn't be made from home. I got in the Explorer, motored back up Route 1, and pulled over at a pay phone outside a Dunkin Donuts.

The same female voice politely identified Saint Joseph's Elementary School. I inquired as to when the next meeting of the Parents Club would take place and was told that it would be on Monday night at seven.

After getting back in the car and driving up the road a mile or so, I stopped at the next payphone and punched in the same number again. This time I deepened my voice and spoke more slowly. "Hi, Matt Fitzgerald of the Ipswich Chronicle. I'm doing a piece on young teachers in the North Shore area—you know, first, second, third year. Do you think there's anybody at Saint Joseph's that fits that description and wouldn't mind talking to me?"

When it comes to being competitive, football coaches have nothing on school administrators. If teachers from other schools were going to be featured in the newspaper, you could bet those from Saint Joseph's would be in there too. "Well, Mr. Hanley would be a fine candidate for you, but he's in class right now. Can I have him call you back?"

I tried to sound slightly embarrassed. "Unfortunately, I forgot my cell this morning and I'm on the road. What time will he be out of class?"

"Twelve o'clock sharp. He usually goes to lunch then, but if you can call back at exactly that time, I'll try to arrange it so that he'll be available for you."

"I wouldn't think of having him miss his lunch," I said. "May I ask what Mr. Hanley's first name is?"

"Joshua."

"Twelve o'clock then. Thank you."

I drove by Wakefield High School to learn the location of the baseball field, and then took a drive through the Breakheart Wildlife Reservation just to pass the time.

At twelve noon I was at yet another different pay phone out on Route 1. I gave Joshua Hanley a minute to get from his class to the office before placing the call. The same woman answered and then handed him the phone.

After introducing myself and repeating the point of my purported mission, I told Hanley I wanted to interview him away from the older teachers and suggested a bagel shop out on Route 1. He said he didn't have another class until two and agreed to meet me in fifteen minutes.

When I spotted the silver Honda Civic, I got out of my car and was waiting to shake his hand as he emerged from his own. He appeared to be a fit, clean-cut young man—blue-striped button down oxford under darkish blond hair and blue eyes.

"Matt Fitzgerald," I professed.

"Josh Hanley." He looked me square in the eye and smiled confidently while firmly grasping my hand.

"Thanks for agreeing to meet with me," I said as we started across the lot.

"My pleasure. So exactly what is it you're interested in finding out?"

"Essentially two things," I told him. "One, who are the young people going into the profession these days and, two, what have you experienced so far. You know, how do the students react to a young teacher, how do the *older* teachers react to a young teacher." I smiled agreeably while I held the door for him.

We ordered our bagel sandwiches—roast beef for him, turkey for me, and then took our seats at a table away from the window.

"So how many years have you been teaching for?"

"This is my fourth. All at Saint Joseph's. Math." He chomped into his sandwich.

"Tell me about it," I urged. "How does what you've experienced compare with what you expected beforehand?" I laid my memo pad on the table and wrote "4 yrs."

I assured Josh that I would leave any negatives he might

have to offer anonymous. After all, I would be visiting with teachers from about half a dozen schools in the general area, so no one would have to know from whence came a particular criticism.

By the time we finished our sandwiches, Josh had told me what I already knew about going into teaching right out of college. Despite my assurance of anonymity, though, he was decidedly reluctant to convey anything too negative about the faculty, the students, their parents, or the school in general. But that was no surprise. Despite my having asked for a first, second, or third year teacher, I was given someone in his fourth year—someone hand picked by the woman who answered the phone in the office. Joshua Hanley was the image Saint Joseph's wanted to project, and he wasn't going to say anything they wouldn't want him to say.

Finally, when the perfunctory stuff was out of the way, I tried to subtly get down to business. "How about the other young teachers at Saint Joseph's. What have they had to say about *their* experiences?"

"Anyone in particular?" he asked.

"Well since I don't know any of them, why don't you start with whoever you want."

"Brittany came the same year I did," he explained. "She teaches biology and chemistry. She's getting married in June. Other than that there's just Brian. He's in his first year. History."

"How about interests outside of work. What do you and Brittany and Brian do when you're not teaching school?"

"Well I swim, play tennis, and ski." He smiled almost apologetically. "I like being outdoors. Brittany, she and her boy friend are into hiking and climbing, and Brian..." Josh paused and seemed to be deciding whether or not he wanted to say something.

"Brian?" I prompted.

He smiled again and diplomatically settled for, "Brian's a pretty keep to himself kind of guy. But he does play in a rock band. They do mostly mellow stuff. He plays bass."

I scribbled on my pad and said, "That sounds like something I could follow up on. Do you know where his band is working right now?"

"Sorry, I don't. We went to see them in Beverly once back in the winter, but I have no idea where they are now?"

"Do you know the name of the band?"

He pointed at me and said, "Odessa."

I looked at him. "I wonder why?"

"Who knows," he said dismissively.

I nodded agreeably, pocketed my pen, and picked up the memo pad. "Do you think Brittany and Brian would agree to talk to me?"

"Ah… when?"

"After school? Maybe tomorrow?"

He thought for a moment. "Well, I'm pretty sure Brittany will, but Brian's been out all week. I doubt that he'll come back on a Friday."

Trying to appear only casually interested, I asked, "Oh, what happened? Is he okay?"

"Yeah, I guess so. I mean I haven't heard. I guess he's just out sick or something."

I didn't believe him, but I nodded.

"By the way, you mentioned that Brittany was getting married. How about you? Are you involved in a relationship of any kind?"

"I'm seeing a couple of women. Nothing that serious yet."

"And Brian?"

He chuckled a bit before answering. "Like I said, Brian pretty much keeps to himself."

As we were getting up to leave, Josh asked, "So when's this going to be in the paper?"

"Well first I've got to run it by my editor, see what he thinks. If he likes it, it'll probably be the week after next."

In the parking lot, I thanked him and told him I'd give him a heads-up before the article ran, if in fact it did. He thanked me in return and we parted with another handshake.

Once back in the car, I opened the memo pad, printed "ODESSA" in all caps and circled it. It was the only thing I got, but it was better than nothing.

I thought I'd try the Wakefield High baseball field again, but it was still empty. I pulled over and called Peter.

"All squeaky clean," he reported. "Who's Carol Svenson anyway?"

"The one I had a date with. I assumed she gave me her maiden name. Said she was from Minnesota."

"Svenson. Sounds Scandinavian."

"And outside of Scandinavia, where are there more Scandinavians than in Minnesota?"

"Exactly," he said. "Too perfect. She was laughing at you."

"Not necessarily," I insisted. "It's a fact that many people of Scandinavian extraction hail from Minnesota."

"Your ass hails from Minnesota."

Why bother? I thanked him for running the check and was about to hang up when he got in, "Wait, let me guess. Jill Perrin is from Paris."

I didn't bother to say goodbye. And I certainly didn't let him know that he'd made me laugh.

The Lakeside Pharmacy was actually in the center, about a block up from the lake. It wasn't one of the big chains; it was an old fashioned privately owned place sandwiched between a music shop and a hair salon. I got the impression that it had been there for a long time, but nevertheless, it looked immaculate and quite respectable. I didn't know whether or not the doctor's younger son would be back to work yet, but I was already in the neighborhood so why not give it a shot.

A tall, stocky man probably pushing thirty stood behind the counter. He was dressed in the prerequisite long white cotton jacket and looked up at me without comment when I entered. The light brown hair and apparent age gave me the impression that he might in fact be Tim Bradley.

I fidgeted around at the over-the-counter cold remedies, reading one box and then another, until I finally gave up and solicited the expertise of the resident pharmacist. Breathing through my mouth and trying to sound congested, I said, "Excuse me. What's the difference between a decongestant and an antihistamine?"

"Are you stuffed up or is it running?" he asked without a smile.

"I think it was more stuffed up this morning, but now it seems to be starting to drip," I claimed.

He came out from behind the counter, took something off the shelf, handed it to me, and returned to behind the counter without speaking. I studied the package for a minute, trying to decide how likely it was that I was going to get my $7.99 worth. I was still deciding when I walked up to the counter and reached for my wallet.

"Dom Rossi," I professed. "I won't shake your hand…" I pointed at my allegedly stuffed nose.

That seemed to loosen him up a bit and he cracked a smile. A small one. "Nice to meet you, Mr. Rossi," he said while he took my ten.

I smiled back and nodded. "I'm new in town. Just learning where to buy a loaf of bread and some cold medication."

"Well, I'm glad you found us," he offered unconvincingly. He handed me the little white bag containing the medicine and slid my change across the counter.

$7.99 wasn't a lot, but it was enough that I had to push

it. "You don't see many of these privately owned drugstores anymore. Have you been here a long time?"

He screwed the cap onto a plastic bottle and didn't look at me when he answered. "The place itself is twelve years older than I am," he said. "But as for me? I just bought it two years ago." Although his response was cordial enough, I found him to be rather cold. Of course he'd just buried his father two days ago.

The door opened and a woman with two young children entered.

Before turning to leave, I offered, "Nice meeting you."

Tim Bradley ignored me and focused on the customer that had just come in.

I drove back to the city half hoping that someone I knew would catch a cold soon. Arriving home shortly before three, I was both surprised and disappointed that Cedric wasn't there to greet me. By the time I crossed the floor to the answering machine, I was a bit pissed off. Ms. Doucette was definitely taking this thing a bit too far.

The lone message on the machine had been waiting there for over three hours.

"Dean!" Nicole sounded animated. "Call me as soon as you get this. Please." She didn't sound angry. It seemed more like there was some matter of urgency that she needed to tell me about.

I punched in her cell number. When she answered I asked, "Where are you?"

"Funny you should ask," she said. In contrast to her tone of three hours earlier, she now sounded weary. "I'm at the State Police barracks on Soldiers Field Road. Can you guess why?"

"Where is he?" I blurted out.

"He's still here with me. He's fine," she said. "But you

have to get over here to confirm what I told them. I'm due in work in only an hour."

I jumped back in Peter's Explorer and headed west on Storrow Drive. "You have to confirm what I told them." *Great. Now all I need to know is what you told them.*

Due to traffic, I didn't arrive until almost quarter past. The trooper at the desk looked up at me and inquired with his eyes only.

"Dean Cello."

"Ah, Mr. Cello. We've been expecting you." He picked up the phone and said, "Cello's here." After whoever was on the other end responded, the guy at the desk put the phone back down and said, "Lieutenant Vieira will be right with you."

Not a minute had passed when a not-too-tall but well-built man in a gray suit approached and introduced himself as Lieutenant Vieira. His white hair was brushed back. I figured him to be late forties, maybe fifty. "This way, Mr. Cello," he ordered with what I took to be a smile of amusement.

After we'd turned a couple of corners, I spotted Nicole sitting on a chair beside a desk and I could see that a female trooper was crouched down on the floor beside her, scratching Cedric. When we got to within twenty feet or so, Cedric noticed me approaching and jumped away from the woman who'd been scratching him and let out a thunderous bark. His tail was wagging frantically and Nicole had to pull on the leash to restrain him.

I dropped to my knees in front of him and let him lick my face. "My best pal," I said to him. After a quick scratch behind his ear, I got up and gave Nicole a kiss on the top of her head. "So what's going on?" I asked.

Nicole did her best to try to look upbeat, but she'd been sitting there for over three hours. "Just tell Lieutenant Vieira the story, okay, Dean. I'm sorry, but I really have to get to work."

Lieutenant Vieira sat at the edge of the desk grinning and waiting.

I started all the way back at Dr. Connor Bradley's phone call and quickly but carefully went up through me finding the dog in Brian's condo unit.

Vieira appeared to be more amused than anything else. When I finished, he yawned and said, "Good night, folks." He then turned to Nicole and added, "Nice meeting you, Ms. Doucette."

"Same here, Ray," she answered.

Ray?

Was I leaving with the dog? No arrest? Not even a fine? I was dying to know, but I didn't want to risk changing the way things seemed to be going.

Once outside, I turned to Nicole and asked, "What's going on?"

She looked exhausted but amused. What was everyone so amused about?

"Drive me to work and I'll tell you all about it," she said.

The three of us climbed into the Explorer.

"Remember when I took Cedric out for a second walk this morning?" she started.

I listened attentively while she explained that she and Cedric had been walking up Comm. Ave. when a State Police car stopped and a plainclothesman flashed a badge and asked her whose dog she was walking. What could she do? Another cop was in the car too; they took her in for questioning with the dog. When they arrived at the station, the cop who'd flashed the badge telephoned Ellen Bradley, who, almost two hours later, finally showed up with her son Kevin. The Bradleys then confirmed that the dog was indeed Sir Cedric of Winchester.

Nicole interrupted her own story to share an observation. "I think you rash judged Ellen," she said. "Once you get passed that pretentious defense, she's really a very nice person."

I looked at her.

"Well we all have our own way of coping," she maintained. "Anyway..."

She went on to explain that when Ellen and Kevin arrived, she asked Lieutenant Vieira if she could explain to them in his presence how Sir Cedric had come into her possession. The lieutenant agreed and Nicole then told her story, essentially *my* story, for the second time. Before she had finished, Kevin shook his head and got up and walked away, but Ellen seemed fascinated. The two talked for a while and Mrs. Bradley eventually expressed that she was "touched" that someone, yours truly, would care so much about a person he didn't even know.

I couldn't stand it anymore. "That's fine, but how about my dog?" I demanded, only half joking.

"*Your* dog?"

I had to pull over. All I could do was stare at her. Finally, she couldn't contain it anymore; she started laughing as hard as I'd ever seen her laugh before.

"Ellen Bradley sold you the dog." I speculated. "How much?" I figured if a used teacart was worth three thousand, Cedric must be worth at least five.

Nicole stopped laughing and looked at me sympathetically. "Have you forgotten about Brian?" she asked.

Of course I momentarily had.

"He's yours until Brian is found," she explained.

"Oh," was all I could offer.

As I started out into traffic again, I asked, "Speaking of Brian, did Ellen Bradley happen to share any ideas with you?"

"Why don't you ask her yourself?" said Nicole. "You've got a luncheon date with her tomorrow—her place at noon."

Chapter 10

I dropped Nicole off at the Channel 3 studio, and then took Cedric home and gave him his dinner. As soon as he was finished, I grabbed the leash and off we went again. It was great not to have to worry about being seen with him. We strolled the Public Gardens and the Common before cutting behind the State House and descending the other side of Beacon Hill toward Storrow Drive. When we reached the esplanade, I repeatedly threw the ball as far as I could and Cedric chased it down with a vengeance and returned it every time. His high energy level was probably due to the fact that he'd been pent up all day at the police station. Afterward, we just sat on the grass for a while and watched the sailboats gliding by on the Charles.

We arrived back at the apartment too late for Nicole's early report, but she'd be doing it again at ten. I spread some fresh parmesan and mozzarella over a formerly frozen pizza crust and popped it in the oven.

We picked up the ballgame in the third inning. I ate the pizza; Cedric laid a few feet away on the floor and crunched on a Nylabone. When I got up to bring the one remaining slice of pizza back into the kitchen, he got up too and followed me. Then when I returned to the study, he did the same, again lying on the carpet, this time while I sat at the computer and updated my notes on the Bradley matter.

A while later, I got up from the computer, and again Cedric got up too. I grabbed the pull toy Nicole had bought him a couple of days ago and we wrestled on the floor for a while.

The Sox won nine to three; it was their fourth in a row, which brought them up to .500. The game ended before the news came on, so we got to see Nicole, looking remarkably refreshed, do the late report.

As usual, Nicole arrived home just a few minutes before eleven. She insisted on taking Cedric out for his five-minute pre-going-to-bed walk. When she returned, I had the wine poured, the TV off, and the light from the table lamp at its lowest setting. As we began chatting in the quiet of the study, it became apparent that the events of the day must have allowed Nicole to put our breakfast conversation in perspective. Later I couldn't help but give myself a mental pat on the back as I did indeed turn the corner and pass Go. We guys are awful.

On Saturday morning, as Cedric was watching me slip on my sweatshirt, I got the idea that maybe he'd like to join me on my run. I let him come along, and he appeared to enjoy himself until we climbed the steps of the Dartmouth Street Bridge, at which point he seemed to tucker out. In deference to my furry friend, I slowed down more than usual for the last half-mile or so.

When I arrived back home, Nicole informed me that Peter had called while I was out. He was going fishing with his future father-in-law again, and he'd worked until the wee hours before it dawned on him that he'd be needing his SUV.

I showered and dressed quickly, then chose chinos instead of jeans despite the fact that it was a Saturday. I had to look my best for Ellen Bradley. The cuffs of the pale blue oxford were still unbuttoned as I tucked in the tails while running out the door.

When I pulled up to Peter's house, he was on the lawn, fishing gear in hand. The moment he spotted me, he started walking toward the car. "I'm going to have a day off sometime toward the end of next week," he said. "Today I'll mention to Frank that you want to come along next time."

"Sounds good," I said. I had never met Linda's father, but I'd always found Linda to be pleasant enough, so I figured her father would most likely be okay too.

"I've got to get Frank. I'm already late," Peter said as we swapped keys.

Peter had already driven off and I was just about to do the same when Linda dashed out of the front door in a bathrobe, arms waving to get my attention. I turned off the engine.

"Nicole's on the phone," she called. "I told her I'd try to catch you."

Linda is tall, with flowing dark hair and eyes to match, but upon meeting her for the first time, what one is most struck by is her extraordinarily dry sense of humor. On this particular occasion it occurred to me that, come October, she was going to need it. I thanked her for chasing me down, went into the house, and asked Nicole what was up.

"Don't bother coming back through the tunnel," she said. "Lieutenant Schmidlin wants to see you at the Peabody barracks."

I warned Nicole that it might be *her* turn to rescue *me*.

After I hung up, Linda and I exchanged pleasantries. I suggested she must be pleased that Peter and her father got along so well. "Oh, it's so great," she said. "They go fishing together. I don't have to bother with either of them." She explained that she was waiting for her friend Marie; the two usually did one of the malls on Saturday morning. I wished her a better day than it appeared I was about to have and pointed the Z4 toward Lynnfield.

By the time I got to the State Police barracks, I'd decided that I couldn't just continue to play *de*fense with Schmidlin. If I did, he would simply continue to hound me mercilessly in the hope that I'd eventually capitulate. Besides, if he had anything on me, he'd be arresting me, and if he didn't, what did I have to lose.

He was standing, talking to the trooper at the desk when

I walked in. Short sleeve khaki shirt, no tie. It was Saturday. It occurred to me that he'd dressed down and I'd dressed up. He looked over at me and pretended to smile.

"How'd you enjoy your donuts?" he asked cheerfully.

I immediately thought of Lou's. "Hey, you should have joined us," I told him with equal enthusiasm.

"Nah," he said. "You just made the call from there. You had lunch at Sunshine Bagel."

Joshua Hanley.

"But have one of mine," he offered. He took a plain out of the box on the front desk and then motioned for me to follow him. There were no sugared crullers. I selected a chocolate frosted and walked behind.

"I'm impressed," I admitted as he closed his office door behind us.

He gave me a satisfied look while taking his seat behind the desk. Suddenly he seemed to notice that only one of us had coffee. Motioning to the front desk, he said, "Why don't you go out and get yourself something to wash that down with."

Seeing as I had to rush out for Peter, I hadn't had my coffee yet, so I took him up on the offer.

I had just walked back through the door when he said, "So what else did you leave out when we last spoke?" I was still thinking when he added, "Besides the fact that you broke into Brian Bradley's condo unit and stole the dog."

"Absolutely nothing, Bob." I bit into my donut.

Schmidlin had carefully laid his own donut down on a napkin at the corner of his desk. He broke off a small piece, put it in his mouth, chewed, and swallowed. "Breaking and entering—that's a crime," he said. "So's theft. A pedigree champion… that could be *grand* theft." He took a sip of his coffee. "And that's not to mention the obstruction of justice." He held his mug in both hands and smiled smugly while waiting for my reaction.

I was curious. "How did you find out I was at Sunshine Bagel?"

He exhaled sharply before answering. "Mr. Cello, eventually, I find out everything." He paused just long enough. "I'm good."

"No, really," I beckoned. "How did you find it out?"

He stared for a moment and then decided to simply dismiss the question with a quick headshake. "It's Saturday, and I've been in this business too long to be here on a Saturday," he said. "I should be on the golf course right now. But I'm not because…" He stopped and appeared to make another decision before continuing. "Because some amateur PI wanna-be is impeding one of my investigations."

"That son of a bitch," I said while shaking my head in disgust. I threw him a confused expression. "But exactly how is it that he has… *impeded* your investigation, Bob?"

Schmidlin snorted. "You know, Dean," he started more pleasantly, "If anyone wanted to press charges, you'd be under arrest right now."

I took another bite of my donut and held up a wait-a-minute finger while I chewed and swallowed. Then just when I was sure he expected me to speak, I washed it down. Finally, I speculated, "But apparently nobody wants to press charges?"

He smiled amusedly and gently nodded. "You're out of your league here, Cello," he warned. He carefully broke another tiny piece off the donut that was still resting atop the napkin. "I want to know everything you know and I want to know it now." He deposited the piece of donut into his mouth.

I looked at him curiously. "I've never seen… a *man*… eat a donut that way," I said.

Without warning, he sprang forward and pounded the desk with his fist, causing the rest of his donut to bounce onto the floor. He didn't look at it, but he knew it had happened. And he knew I knew. And he knew I knew he knew. His face turned crimson. I almost felt guilty. In fact I did feel guilty. Just a little.

"Look, Lieutenant," I offered contritely, "we both know that as long as I don't hide evidence or misrepresent myself as a police officer or otherwise do something illegal, you can't keep me from investigating." I smiled agreeably. "Besides, if I'm such an amateur, what are you so worried about?"

Schmidlin made a nice recovery; he even ignored the donut on the floor. "You might be an amateur, Dean, but I know you're not a stupid man. I'm an officer of the law conducting a homicide investigation and the last time I interviewed you, you lied to me."

"Well first of all," I started, "when we last met, you didn't tell me you were conducting a homicide investigation and you didn't tell me I was being interviewed. In fact you were pretty vague about the whole thing. You said you just wanted to talk as one professional to another. In fact you told me to call you Bob. Secondly, as far as an obstruction of justice charge goes, we both know that you're not going anywhere with that unless you can demonstrate harm. Without harm, the only thing that's been impeded is your Saturday morning trip to the golf course. And if I may be so audacious as to point it out, sir, that was your call."

He hated me. It occurred to me that I must be a sick bastard because I was loving having him hate me.

After he studied me for an appropriate length of time, he suggested, "Let's not talk semantics." He got up and began to pace while continuing. "In fact, let me get right down to it. I am indeed conducting a homicide investigation and I am right this moment interviewing you relative to that investigation."

"Ah," I said, as though enlightenment had arrived. "And am I a suspect?"

He didn't want to say no but he couldn't say yes. "No," he finally conceded.

"Good. Then I don't need my lawyer. So what can I do for you, Bob?"

"You can tell me what you've learned," he suggested. It was definitely a suggestion.

I didn't have to fake the chuckle. "I haven't learned anything," I told him.

He didn't believe me but what could he do? The funny thing was it was essentially true.

Schmidlin stepped closer with both hands in his pockets and just looked at me for a moment. Then, softly, he said, "If I find out you've been sheltering a suspect..." He nodded ominously, indicating the obvious. "We're talking murder here."

I thought for a moment before answering. When I did answer, I tried to do so as seriously and as convincingly as possible. "I'm not sheltering anyone, Lieutenant Schmidlin. And if I may say so, I'd never be that stupid."

Although he'd never let on, I felt that he sensed my sincerity. He turned and headed back behind his desk. "Have a nice day, Dean," he offered.

"You too, Lieutenant," I said as I got up and started for the door. But then there was something I had to know. "Josh—"

"The woman who answers the phone at the school. After Hanley got back and told her about the interview, she called the Ipswich Chronicle." Obviously pleased with himself, he actually smiled affably as he gave me a "Get out of here."

A check of my watch revealed that I was still about an hour early for my luncheon date with Ellen Bradley. Since I hadn't had a chance to see the paper yet, I drove into Lynnfield center and bought the *Globe*. Then I moved down the street to Lou's Donut Shop, where I planned to read the news over a cup of coffee while I waited for noon to roll around.

I had just taken a seat when I overheard a couple of old-timers at the table behind me. I'd just walked passed them—two guys in plaid shirts.

"Yeah, the newspaper said it was an accident, but Jimmy says the police are investigating it."

I opened to page 2, folded the paper, and pretended to read.

"Does seem funny," the other said. "Guy's been takin' a swim every night for how long, then all of a sudden he doesn't know where the bottom is?"

"Somethin' happened there," the first guy agreed. "You know, the nephew teaches up at Saint Joe's. Ain't been in all week. Nothing odd about that under the circumstances, 'cept I heard he never called."

The other guy snorted. "We ain't heard the end of this one yet."

The conversation shifted to someone who'd taken a heart attack. I turned to the next page and didn't read that one either. The two old-timers had caused me to again focus on what Schmidlin had said.

"If I find out you've been sheltering a suspect..." I was surprised to hear him say that, because I had explained to him in our first meeting how Brian was the one who'd come to me, fearful that someone was out to get his uncle. But in order to be sheltered you've got to be missing, and Brian was the only one missing.

I managed to get through the sports page before it was time to head over to Ellen Bradley's house.

It had occurred to me that there was at least a possibility that Carol's car would be there, in which case I would have to pass up the luncheon opportunity. But as it turned out, the driveway was clear, at least for the time being.

As I stood under the portico and rang the bell, I was reminded that it had been a week to the day since I met Brian there and looked at the oaks trees.

Upon opening the door, Ellen Bradley displayed an

expression that I took to be both empathetic and patronizing. “Come in, Mr. Cello,” she offered while extending one arm in the direction of the foyer. She was neatly dressed in an off-white shirt with a moss green lightweight cable-knit sweater and beige pleated chinos.

“Thank you, Mrs. Bradley. Nice of you to have me. And please, call me Dean.” Any reciprocal invitation of informality was conspicuously absent. But she did smile pleasantly while escorting me to the formal room—the one with the Sorrento teacart.

I sat at one end of the mostly-blue calico chintz sofa, adjacent to the chair in which I expected she would seat herself. As soon as I was off my feet, though, she said, “Excuse me. I’ll be right back,” and headed off in the direction of the kitchen. The cherry coffee table in front of the sofa had on it a serving tray with an elegant pewter teapot, matching creamer and sugar bowl, and two teaspoons. It looked as though it had been arranged to be photographed.

Not half a minute later, Mrs. Bradley returned smiling, carrying a plate in both hands. “I made tuna salad and there’s also turkey with your choice of cheeses, Swiss or American.” She placed the sandwiches down beside the teapot. They were all made with white bread and neatly sliced in half from corner to corner.

Again I thought she was about to seat herself, but instead she opened a small wooden box from which I was to select the particular tea that suited my fancy. I chose Lemon Lift because it was the first one facing me.

Mrs. Bradley selected something that wasn’t Lemon Lift and then did the honors of pouring the steaming water. That task completed, she turned and headed toward the adjacent chair. I noticed again how fit she was. Finally, she sat down.

“Mr. Cello, I want to tell you that I was very touched,” she began. “When Nicole ever explained to me all that you were trying to accomplish for someone you don’t even know…”

Legs together and to one side, she held her saucer in one hand and the handle of the teacup in the other. She shook her head and gazed at me admiringly.

"I was only in the doctor's presence for less than an hour," I said, "but I could tell he was a wonderful man."

"But you never even deposited the check he gave you," she marveled. "Naturally, with all that was going on, I didn't give it a thought, but after Nicole explained it all, I called the bank and..." Again she smiled at me admiringly.

"I had planned to return the check to you today, Mrs. Bradley, but as it turned out, I had to leave the house in a hurry this morning. A friend of mine—"

"Don't you worry about it, Mr. Cello. Please... have a sandwich. I made them just for you."

I'd just had turkey with Josh Hanley yesterday, so I selected a tuna salad. How bad could it be? I took a small bite, chewed, and swallowed. "This might well be the best tuna sandwich I've ever tasted," I told her. In fact that statement wasn't far from the truth. The piece of work had a great bod *and* she made a mean sandwich.

"I'm glad you're enjoying it," she said. She delicately took a sip of her tea. "I love Nicole," she beamed. "Whenever Dan Harding goes on vacation... I enjoy her so much. She looks so clean."

"That she does, Mrs. Bradley. I love her too."

Ellen Bradley initiated a conversation about a couple of the human-interest stories that constituted Nicole's regular assignment at Channel 3.

"She just this past Sunday returned from doing a piece about the dying timber industry up in northern Maine," I told her. "I think she said it was going to run in two parts, probably next week."

This was all fine, but I had a lot of questions to ask and I assumed that my welcome time was limited.

We both sipped our tea at the same time and then Mrs.

Bradley spoke again. "Nicole said there were some questions you would probably want to ask me, Mr. Cello. About… you know… Connor."

So she had simply been making pleasantries, giving us both enough time to get comfortable with one another before getting down to business.

"I was somewhat apprehensive about bringing it up," I admitted. "I don't want to be offensive in any way."

She dismissed my concerns with a wave of her hand. "After all the questions we endured at the hands of the police…" She rolled her eyes. "Please, Mr. Cello. Feel free."

There was no pretty way to do this, so I figured I'd just go right to the heart of the matter. "I believe Nicole mentioned to you that Brian attempted to retain my services because he suspected that someone wanted to harm your husband."

"Harm him? You mean kill him, Mr. Cello."

"Yes," I acknowledged rather sheepishly. "And I've been feeling terribly guilty about having dismissed Brian as a young man with an overactive imagination."

"Nonsense," she tried to assure me. "Why would you have given any serious consideration to such an outlandish idea?"

"So you don't believe that your husband was…" I hoped I didn't have to say it.

"Murdered?" she obliged. She continued to smile as she exaggeratedly shook her head from one side to the other. "Absolutely not. Why would anyone want to murder Connor? Everybody loved him. Everybody."

"Well I have to admit that he did seem like an easy person to love," I said. I thought I'd try taking a step sideways. "And of course, then there's the matter of Brian. Does anyone know where he is?"

Mrs. Bradley took a deep breath before responding. "I'm afraid that remains a mystery so far," she acknowledged. "But Brian was very close to his Uncle Connor. After his mother died, he lived with us from the time he was ten years old until he went off to college. Back when he was only six, his father went to work one day and never returned. Nobody's ever found out for sure what happened to him either. Anyway, as an only child, Brian had it perhaps more difficult than most. But Connor… he always took whatever time was necessary to ensure that Brian would develop the self-confidence necessary to survive in the world." She gazed down at the oriental carpet. "But I don't know that he ever has," she added.

I didn't know how it mattered, but I was curious. "How did his mother die?" I asked.

"Brain aneurysm."

I nodded. "What are his interests? I know he plays the bass, but is there anything else?"

Mrs. Bradley shrugged. "He minored in history. He was especially interested in Russian studies. In fact I remember him doing a paper on the reign of Ivan the Terrible."

Odessa.

I thought I'd try going back to the doctor. "So you say the police asked all of you a lot of questions concerning Dr. Bradley's…" It happened again.

"Yes," she graciously picked up. "I certainly wouldn't classify myself as a television person by any stretch of the imagination… other than the news of course… but I have watched enough to know that family members are always the chief suspects when murder is suspected."

"But you don't believe that that's what happened to Dr. Bradley."

"No, I don't, but apparently the *police* do." She emitted a hint of a laugh. "Utterly preposterous," she exclaimed.

"So then in all that questioning, they must have asked everyone where he or she was when the accident happened."

"Oh, Lord, yes. Several times, each one of us. I finally had to telephone the Chief of the State Police. 'I don't pay taxes to get harassed,' I told him."

I smiled as agreeably as I knew how and softly implored, "If you would be so kind, Mrs. Bradley, I promise I'll only ask you once."

She let out an exasperated, "Oh," but then said, "Well, what's one more time?" She placed the cup and saucer down on the table and asked me if I'd like more tea. I declined the tea but told her I wouldn't mind another half sandwich. That seemed to please her. She gave me a "Please do," and then sat perfectly straight again, clasped her hands together on her lap, and began to recite it all as if by rote.

Since the doctor had made plans to accompany his eldest son to look at a piece of property up in New Hampshire that morning, he and the Mrs. had refrained from scheduling any social engagements that evening. The doctor's sixtieth birthday was coming up in a couple of weeks, so Ellen Bradley decided she would go to the North Shore Mall while her husband took his nightly swim. They had planned to later spend a quiet evening at home watching a rented movie. During the course of the investigation, the police had requested and received the sales slip for a shirt and tie Ellen Bradley had purchased at Brooks Brothers. Of course that wasn't his big gift, just a little something on the side.

Tim, the Bradleys' younger son, had gone with a friend to see Brian's band, but of course Brian ended up not being there. Tim and his friend stayed for a while and then went home.

The two daughters-in-law, Carol and Jill, went to a movie together. Ellen Bradley wasn't sure what the title was, but it was something that neither of their husbands was interested in seeing.

Tired from having gotten up so early and from having taken the long ride, Kevin remained home alone, planning to watch something on the Discovery Channel and expecting to fall asleep before it was over. In fact when Ellen Bradley called him to report the awful news, he was awakened from his slumber on a chair in the family room.

The police had gone over everything with each of them in great detail.

When it seemed that Ellen Bradley was all talked out, I thanked her and asked if I could ask just a few more questions.

"Why not?" she said.

"Were you still home when Brian called to report that he had the dog?"

"Yes. Connor was so happy to hear that Cedric was all right. He couldn't wait to see him."

"But then Brian never showed up?"

"Oh, no, he did. He came over right after he called. Mid-afternoon sometime."

Understandably, I was confused. "But when the accident happened, Cedric wasn't here. Is that right?"

"Well I don't know," she said. "All I'm certain of is that he was here when I left for the Mall and he wasn't here when I returned." I digested that for a moment before moving on.

"Did Tim mention whether or not the band had a replacement bass player?"

"I'm sorry, Mr. Cello, I don't know about that. In fact I've essentially told you everything I know at this point. Just like I did with the police."

If that wasn't an invitation to leave, I'd never heard one. I came to my feet. "Thank you so much, Mrs. Bradley. This must all still be very difficult for you. I certainly appreciate your time, your patience, and your excellent tuna salad sandwiches."

There were still a couple of things I wanted to know; I figured I'd try to take care of them on the way to the door.

"You know, it must have been tough on your own sons having another sibling of sorts to share their dad with."

"Well, that's true. Especially Tim, probably because he was the younger one. He was still in high school when we took Brian in and of course Connor wanted to do all that he could for the poor boy, so there was bound to be some jealousy. But it all worked out in the end."

I stopped in the middle of the foyer and turned to face Ellen Bradley. "Mrs. Bradley, other than the obvious, did you notice anything unusual, anything different, in or around the house when you returned from the Mall that night?"

"Now you sound like that police lieutenant," she said almost playfully.

"Schmidlin?"

"Yes. What an awful man. He tries to convince you that he's compassionate while all the time he's hoping you'll say something that will give him justification to arrest you. But of course I was joking; you're nothing at all like him. I could tell by the way you placed the napkin on your lap and you knew exactly what to do with your spoon. You're obviously the product of a proper upbringing, Mr. Cello. And I'll bet you'll find Brian before that silly buffoon does."

"That means a lot to me coming from you, Mrs. Bradley. Thank you very much."

As she held the door, she added, "Please say hello to Nicole for me. And if there's anything else you need, do feel free to let me know."

You and me, Ellen.

Chapter 11

While driving out to Route 1, I pulled Nicole up on her cell. Before I could get a word in, she said, "Oh, I was hoping you'd call. Linda called here looking for you. She needs some help with the lawnmower."

"Did you say the *lawnmower*?"

"Yeah. I told her that if you called I'd ask you to go by on your way home."

Interesting. "Okay, I will. But in the meantime, can you do me a huge favor? I need to find out where a rock band named Odessa is playing tonight. Most likely somewhere on the North Shore. Would you be so wonderful as to go online or open the phone book and start hunting for me?"

"Does this mean we're going clubbing tonight?"

"Well either *we* are or *I* am. But I'd enjoy it much more if you were with me, my love."

Nicole agreed to do the search while I went by to see what Linda needed with the lawnmower.

The inside door of the little white cape was open. I called through the screen door.

"Oh, what a guy," Linda said in her typically understated way.

"I thought you were going shopping?"

"Yeah, well something came up with Marie's mom, so she had to go over there. But I figured 'That's okay. If I get rid of the lawn today, I won't have to do it tomorrow,' but then I couldn't get the mower started."

I looked at her and tried to digest what she'd just said. "Tomorrow. As in when Peter's here."

"Yeah." She looked at me blankly for a moment, and

then, without any sign of emotion whatsoever, said, "Oh, I get it. Peter mowing a lawn."

"Who feeds it?" I asked.

Linda looked at me like I'd just grown a third eye. "How long have you known him?" she asked.

I had to take a look at the mower despite the fact that I was sure my brain didn't even *have* a file named "Lawnmowers." But lo and behold, my cursory examination revealed something even I couldn't miss—the sparkplug wire had disconnected. Linda apologized for me having had to go out of my way for something she should have noticed herself. I told her she'd just made my day. It didn't take much to get her to promise not to tell Peter.

By the time I arrived home, Nicole had learned that Odessa was playing at Brandy's in Beverly. I played on the floor with Cedric for a while, and then watched what was left of the ballgame while Nicole fed our furry friend and took him for his post-dinner walk.

After freshening up, we strolled down to Hillary's for dinner. Hillary's can probably best be described as an upscale pub. It was where Nicole and I had our first "date"—an impromptu event that took place last September, when she'd just moved in upstairs and started her new job at Channel 3.

Forty-odd minutes after leaving Hillary's, we arrived at Brandy's. Odessa was somewhere in the middle of the first set, doing a mellow tune that I had never heard before. The band consisted of four rather ordinary looking guys in their mid to late twenties—keyboard, guitar, bass, and drums. The guitar player was singing lead with the keyboard guy joining in here and there on the harmony. Three of the four were wearing long-sleeved jerseys; the bass player sported a work shirt, untucked of course.

There were still a lot of open tables. We selected one near

the bar. Nicole ordered a cosmopolitan and I of course had my amaretto on ice. Since the band continued to do all soft stuff, we were able to sip and chat leisurely. I mentioned Schmidlin threatening me about sheltering a suspect.

"When you stand back and look at it objectively," Nicole said, "it does look suspicious that a murder gets committed and a family member disappears at the same time."

"I guess that's my problem," I said. "I can't disregard that Brian was the one who got me involved. He was the one who was concerned about his uncle's well-being. Schmidlin wasn't in the donut shop with us last Saturday morning. I know first hand how concerned Brian was."

As usual, Nicole played devil's advocate. "Or how concerned he wanted you to think he was."

"Mm, but by all accounts, he's rather shy. I don't see him being so calculatingly devious."

"Would you see him manipulating his uncle into retaining the services of a private investigator?"

It was a fair question, and since I had no answer, I simply nodded my acknowledgement and put it on a shelf. "How about Schmidlin?" I asked. "He can't possibly really think I'm sheltering anyone."

Nicole thought for a moment and then offered, "You always have to ask yourself where a person's real interest lies. For Schmidlin, it's cracking the case, sure, but the reason behind him wanting to do that is the feather in his cap he gets from his superiors."

"Feather in his cap?" I teased.

Nicole tossed her head slightly. "My grandmother used to use it. Anyway, what would it say about him if a novice PI beat him out?"

"So you think he was throwing me a red herring?"

Nicole shrugged and raised her eyebrows, indicating that although she couldn't be sure, the hypothesis might at least be worthy of some consideration. Then she returned to something I'd told her about over dinner. "So Ellen was relaxed today, huh?"

I took a sip of my amaretto before responding to the change in direction. "Even when she talked about coming home and finding her husband. Seems odd for a woman who's been married to the same man for over three decades. You'd think she would have gotten all broken up, assuming she were able to talk about it at all. So soon, I mean."

Nicole's eyes narrowed the way they did when she was doing some serious thinking. "Ellen Bradley is an interesting woman," she decided. "Did you ask her about 'The doctor is dead?'"

I shook my head. "It was a frivolous question anyway so I thought I'd save it till the end, but then when she in effect told me that I'd already asked one too many…"

The music stopped and when we looked around we saw that more than half the tables were now full. The guitar player and the keyboardist went off to an empty table close to the stage, the drummer sat with a young blonde, and the bass player sauntered up to the bar. It was time to go to work.

Nicole came with me. We approached the guitar and keyboard guys all cheerful and upbeat. "Hey, I just want to tell you guys that you're really great," I said.

They both smiled appreciatively. The guitar player gave me a simple, "Thanks."

Nicole jumped in. "Didn't we see you here before? Back in the fall?"

"You're thinking of Jerome's over on Essex Street," the other guy said.

Nicole and I looked at each other. "Okay. Yeah. We've been in there."

"I like that you do a lot of mellow stuff," I told them. "It's kinda different for a club."

The guitar player looked happy to hear that. "Yeah, we like that stuff too, but most of the people that come to these places on a Saturday night want to let go, so in the middle sets we gotta pick it up a bit."

"*Quite* a bit," the other guy said. The two looked at each other and laughed.

"Well we'll just have to hang around for that," Nicole said.

"Yeah," the keyboardist agreed. "That's cool too."

After joining in the reverie some, I gave my slightly confused look. "If I'm not mistaken, didn't you have a different bass player when we last saw you?"

"Brian," they both said, just slightly out of synch.

I nodded and then looked over to make sure the replacement guy wasn't on the way over. He was talking to a young woman at the bar. "Yeah, I thought it wasn't the same guy," I said. "I mean this guy's good too, but I remember the other guy… he had a certain feel."

"Brian's our regular bass player," said Guitar. "He rehearses with us all the time, so you know… that shows."

"So where is he tonight?" I asked.

Both made a few low unintelligible sounds, and then the guitar guy took the lead again. "The truth is, like we don't know where he is."

I faked a minor laugh. "You lost your bass player. So when did that happen?"

Guitar got out only, "Well—" when Keyboard cut him off. "Are you a cop?"

I laughed a little harder. "No," I told him. "I'm not a cop. We just like to make the rounds occasionally and listen to the local bands. You never know when you're gonna see the stars of the future, right? Anyway, as I said before, we really like your sound and… well I just think the other bass player… hey if there's something goin' on that I shouldn't know about…"

"Nah, it's not that," said Guitar. "We're just stressed out about it too." He looked over at Keyboard who was lighting up a cigarette. "Last week we were working here and he just didn't show. No call. Nothing. And Brian's a pretty straight guy, so naturally we're..." He shrugged. "We don't know."

I adopted a more concerned expression. "Wow. I'm sorry."

I'd noticed that Keyboard had been looking at me with narrowed eyes, but suddenly his head turned in the direction of the door? When he looked back at me he was wearing what I took to be a smirk. "Here comes his cousin," he said. "Maybe he can answer your questions." He flipped a thumb in the direction of Tim Bradley, who took two more steps before stopping at the table.

"Questions about what?" Bradley wanted to know.

"This guy's been asking about Brian," said Keyboard, now wearing a smug grin.

Tim Bradley looked down at me. From my seated position, he looked even bigger than he had in the pharmacy. "Hey, I guess the cold's better, huh?"

"Well it was you who picked the medicine," I jovially reminded him. "You're the regular bass player's cousin? I was just telling these guys how much we like their sound, but we knew when we saw them back in the fall, they had a different bass player..."

The replacement bass guy walked over and stood beside Tim Bradley.

I came to my feet and addressed the guitar player. "Well anyway, you guys are great. Someday when you make it big, I'll be able to say I knew you when, huh? Good luck, guys." And with that, Nicole and I initiated what we hoped was a smooth escape.

The place wasn't quite filled to capacity yet and the table we'd abandoned still had our nearly empty glasses on it, so we were able to reclaim it.

Odessa turned up the amps and opened the second set with *Old Time Rock n' Roll.* A lot of folks got up to dance away the cares of the past week.

When the barmaid came around, we ordered two soda waters—Nicole's with lemon, mine with lime. We sipped and listened to the band and tried not to look at Tim Bradley, who was seated at a table toward the back and on the other side of the room.

Eventually, we too got up and danced. I was never much of a dancer, but if Bradley was still watching, I didn't want him to think I was staking him out, which of course I was.

A couple of casual glances in his direction revealed that he had a lot of friends. But of course he was the friendly neighborhood pharmacist. In a town fifteen miles away.

Near the end of the second set, he got up and made his way to the door. Halfway across the floor he turned quickly and caught me looking. I casually raised my glass to him and offered a half smile, which he didn't bother to return. Instead he looked over at Keyboard and gave him a quick wave before heading out the door.

At that point, Nicole and I had had enough, but I wanted to give Tim Bradley a solid head start. We stayed through the break and then got up and left just as the third set was beginning.

The night air had grown chilly and a light fog had rolled in off the ocean. Upon arriving at the car, I was relieved to see that it was still all in one piece. Of course I'd been in the Explorer when I'd left the Lakeside Pharmacy, but Tim's wife Jill had watched me every step of the way last Wednesday as I drove the Z4 out of her gallery lot and back out to Route 127.

Nicole reached behind the seat for the blanket I kept back there, and then wrapped it around herself while I started the engine. As I exited the parking lot, I glanced in the rearview mirror to make sure there wasn't another pair of headlights joining us on the way out. There wasn't. But then, not more than a hundred feet down the road, a couple appeared right behind us, as if out of nowhere. I didn't bother to mention it.

When Nicole spoke, it was obvious that she was shivering. "So either Cousin Tim was hoping Brian would be there, or Cousin Tim came for some other reason altogether."

I turned right onto 1A.

So did the headlights.

"A popular pharmacist and a nightclub. We might have hit upon something," I said.

"And the keyboard player's manner seemed to indicate that Cousin Tim doesn't have a sense of humor. Agreed?"

"Agreed." We drove in silence for a few minutes while Nicole warmed up and I kept one eye in the rearview mirror. The little man in my brain played a recording of Peter advising me to buy a gun. "The day will come when you'll wish you had it." If he'd said it once he'd said it a thousand times.

When we got to Route 62, I took a right. The car behind us did the same.

"You warming up any over there?"

"Yeah, but I'm sure glad you can take Cedric for his walk tonight."

"Thanks, pal."

Two more rights and we were back where we'd started. Our companion was still behind us. I didn't know of any other reason for someone to drive in circles. "Don't turn around, but we're being followed."

Nicole remained silent for a moment, then she looked over at me and said, "This is more excitement than a girl from Derry needs on a Saturday night."

I didn't answer. I was thinking.

Finally, she asked. "What are you going to do?"

"I'm figuring he probably doesn't want to hurt us," I said. "He could have done that in the parking lot. So it must be that he wants to know where I live. Essentially, who I am."

The fog seemed to be getting thicker in the low spots. I nearly missed the sign for 62. This time I turned left and headed west toward the highway. I'd have been surprised if the car behind us had not done the same.

"It was bound to happen eventually," I said. "The Bradleys must talk like any other family. The doctor and his son Kevin went all the way up to Winnipesaukee and back last Saturday. It would have been odd if the father didn't mention to the son that he had hired someone to find his lost dog. Then each of the daughters-in-law and the other son all get a visit from a guy who fits the same description. Not to mention that Kevin got the story from you at the State Police office yesterday afternoon, and then to clinch it, I have lunch with the widow today."

"That all makes sense, but it still doesn't explain why one of them is following you. Why wouldn't he just ask his mother who you were? Is he still behind us?"

"Yeah, but hopefully not for long." I got on the entrance ramp and hit the gas, hoping that whatever he was driving wasn't going to be able to catch the Z4. I made it all the way over to the left as quickly as possible and stomped on it harder still. A quick glance in the mirror revealed that the headlights behind us were getting smaller. As the highway bent to the left, I waited until the lights were out of sight, then quickly looked for an opening, turned off my own lights, and moved all the way over to the right. Then I slowed dramatically and continued to drive without headlights. The fog was much lighter up on the highway and the vehicles around me provided enough light to keep me from driving off the road. Every few seconds I glanced over to see if anyone was driving fast in the left lane. Finally, I caught a light colored Saab go flying by. It came into sight and then was gone again in seconds.

I took the next exit and didn't put the headlights back on until I was on whatever street it was, heading west somewhere in Peabody. Nobody had followed us coming off the highway. We didn't mind taking the long way home.

Chapter 12

According to Nicole, it was necessary to take Cedric only as far as the hydrant that was a mere three doors away. Apparently he never had any additional business to tend to on his late night excursion. Nicole said that after the trip to the hydrant, she always walked him to the corner of Clarendon and back simply because they were already out anyway.

I went out with the intention of doing just as she had recommended, but she was right; it just felt too quick. I cast fate to the wind and walked my canine friend to the corner of Clarendon. While I told myself I was doing so simply because I was already out there, I knew full well that I had another reason as well. In effect, I was telling Tim Bradley that he wasn't going to change my life. Not one iota.

We finished off Saturday night playing on the floor with Cedric and then sipping wine by the fire. We didn't discuss the Bradleys. Any of them.

On Sunday morning, Cedric and I did our run. I showed him the alternate route. It was a cloudy, cool day, more like March than mid-April, but that was okay.

After showering and getting dressed, Nicole and I decided it might be nice to take a ride up the coast to a pancake house we had eaten at back in September when we were first getting acquainted.

The Z4 was parked around the corner on Berkley Street, where we'd left it after taking the back roads home on Saturday night.

Nicole saw it first. She stopped in her tracks, eyes wide and staring. I turned to look and noticed the windshield—

totally smashed in, with the light drizzle that was now falling getting all over the dash and the leather. Then I spotted the four flat tires. Upon closer inspection, it became apparent that the sidewalls had been slashed. And the passenger side door had been keyed. Somehow I didn't think this was a random act of unkindness.

Nicole said exactly what I was thinking. "They already knew where you lived."

"Which makes sense now that Ellen Bradley knows all about me," I conceded. "Like any mother, she wouldn't be able to envision her children doing any wrong. And I do advertise in the phone book."

"So what was with the following us?"

"Intimidation," I ventured. "Looks like we got a little too close to something. Somebody's telling us to back off."

We walked down to Boylston Street and had breakfast at Angels, a place that consistently served decent food but weak coffee. I didn't mean to be quieter than usual; I must have been doing a lot of thinking. Then I recalled something I had once heard and thought I'd share it with Nicole.

"I remember once hearing that when aerial bombing first started, back in World War I, the theory behind it was that the people being attacked right where they lived would cry out for an end to the war at all cost. But interestingly enough, what actually happened was that they became more incensed, more determined to inflict even worse casualties on their enemy."

Nicole smiled dubiously. "You going to smash Tim Bradley's windshield?"

"No," I said. "But this cloak and dagger routine is over. Forget Dave Snell and Matt Fitzgerald et al. Tomorrow morning I'm Dean Cello and I'm gonna kick some ass."

Nicole couldn't contain her laugher. "Is this the *new* Dean Cello?" she asked.

I couldn't help but laugh some myself, but I still meant what I said. "Even nice guys have their limits," I told her.

Becoming more serious, Nicole suggested, "Don't sell Dave Snell and Matt Fitzgerald short. You learned some things you probably wouldn't have learned flashing a PI license." I had to begrudgingly concede that that was probably true.

After leaving Angels, we strolled back to the apartment by way of Newbury Street. At twelve o'clock sharp I called the BMW dealer on Comm. Ave. and made arrangements to have my wreck towed in. I asked about a loaner and was told they would check to see what was available. Ask for Chuck.

We took the Green Line up Comm. Ave. and walked into the showroom. A fashionably dressed, slightly older man pounced on us with measured precision. "May I help you?"

"Dean Cello. I was told to ask for Chuck."

"Chuck Walters," he said, extending a hand. He looked more like a Charles. "I'm afraid we don't have much available at the present time. We've been pretty busy. But I do have what I'm sure you'll agree is civil transportation. It'll get you through the week." He led us out to the used car lot.

Chuck walked passed some decent-looking upscale cars and then stopped suddenly and extended his arm to the side almost apologetically. I felt myself beam. It was a green early nineties Volvo 240. I was home again.

Five minutes later the rain had started falling in earnest as we drove away looking like a couple of schoolteachers.

"I'd forgotten how much I liked these cars," I admitted. "And I bet I could even win a race with a bicycle."

We stopped to pick up a couple of movies on the way back down Comm. Ave. The ballgame was sure to be postponed anyway.

We spent the rest of a lazy Sunday afternoon watching our movies. Cedric occasionally looked up to make sure we were still there, then sighed contentedly before going back to sleep. In the evening we called in a pizza and ate it on the floor by the fireplace.

Monday morning was cloudy, but at least the rain had stopped. My pal and I ran the regular route and he made it all the way through without getting winded. What a guy.

Dan, the regular news anchor, was due to return from his vacation, so that meant Nicole was back on her daytime hours. The Maine timber segment was scheduled to run tonight and tomorrow night. But since I had to be at the Parents Club meeting at seven, we planned to record it and watch it together after I got home. It also occurred to me that my day on the North Shore might run long, so I packed a change of clothes suitable for St. Joseph's. Nicole said she'd be home in time to feed Cedric.

After Nicole left for work, I updated my notes on the Bradley "case." For a while, Cedric sat beside me and rested his chin on my leg.

Before I left I gave my friend a biscuit, a scratch, and a promise that I'd see him later. I told him to guard the house, even though I knew he wouldn't.

My first order of business was a drive-by of the Lakeside Pharmacy in Wakefield. Indeed, there was a silver-blue Saab parked right out in front. I read the registration number into my memo recorder and kept driving. Eventually the Wakefield High baseball team would be either playing or practicing and that was where I wanted to confront him—away from his business and his customers.

I popped in a Duke Robillard CD and drove up the coast to Rockport. It was just after noon when I parked at a meter out on 127 and walked up the side street to the Perrin Art Gallery. It was closed.

Maybe the antique dealer would know. I strolled in and gave him a friendly, "How's it going?"

He greeted me enthusiastically. "Still looking for one of those Sorrento teacarts?"

"I wasn't really looking for one," I confessed. "It was just that I'd met someone who had one and she told me it was her prized possession, so naturally, I wondered."

He smiled agreeably and placed both hands on his sizable midsection. "So what can we do for you today?"

"Well I was hoping to visit the art gallery, but I see she's closed. Do you have any idea why?"

He chuckled a bit and waved his hand dismissively. "You got lucky last time," he said. "More often than not she locks up around lunch time and doesn't come back till about four or so."

"You got any idea where she goes?"

"I told you last week, we don't do much talking." Suddenly, he looked at me skeptically.

Here we go. I took out my wallet and held the PI license up for him to examine.

"I've seen some things, but I don't suppose it's any of my business," he said.

I pointed to the end table beside him. "How much do you want for those candlestick holders?"

"Hundred dollars."

"For a pair of candlestick holders?"

"Those are real fine candlestick holders," he insisted. "Brushed brass, weighted…"

I counted out five twenties and held them close to my chest. "So you were saying—you've seen some things."

He slowly reached over and clamped onto the twenties while explaining. "Gets in a blue car. Some guy with a ponytail. Leaves her own car in the lot here. Then she comes back around four, stays till five, maybe a little later if she's got customers. Been going on for about two months now."

"Do you know what kind of a car?"

He started pocketing the money. "Never paid much attention. Just couldn't help but notice, though."

"Is there anything else you can think of that might be helpful?"

He picked up the candlestick holders and started walking toward the back of the shop. "Nah, I think that about covers it," he said. He stopped at a desk and slowly wrapped my hundred-dollar pre-owned candlestick holders in plain brown paper. Then he neatly taped the paper before handing me the package. No sales slip. I didn't bother to ask.

"Thanks," I said, trying my best to be stoic.

"Those'll look real nice on that Sorrento teacart," he suggested.

I bit my lip and nodded. On the way out I considered that I'd been doing investigations for a year and a half and if I had a dollar for every time I flashed my license and didn't end up paying for it, I'd now have enough to buy lunch.

As it turned out, I spent my own $9.95 for another fisherman's platter at Captain Jack's, but I had to admit it was every bit as outstanding as the one I'd had a week ago.

It was just after two-thirty when I approached the Wakefield High School baseball field and I could see that this time it was indeed occupied. All the kids wore the same uniform—obviously a practice.

I parked behind the backstop and got out to watch. Big Tim Bradley, so far oblivious to my presence, was hitting ground balls and barking instructions to the infielders. They were working on their double play. A good-sized kid in uniform was hitting fungoes to the outfielders.

A solid five minutes went by before an errant throw reached the backstop causing Bradley to look over and notice me. I smiled agreeably. Well maybe a little extra agreeably. He pretended not to notice and went back to work.

While I watched the remainder of the workout, I decided that this was a perfect situation in which to apply the philosophy of the French general—the best defense is a good offense. I wasn't a hundred percent sure that I was basing that assessment more on logic than emotion, but at the moment, it didn't matter.

It was another hour before batting practice ended and the players began to disperse. Bradley took his time talking to a few of them before finally turning to head in my direction. I began strolling toward him as well, and when we met, we were behind a low chain link fence, about halfway between the first base dugout and home plate.

"What do you want?" he asked as though he had better things to do.

I showed him my PI license. He chuckled, looked back up at me and said, "Yeah?"

"How's the drug business?" I asked. Before he could answer I added, "You've been putting in a lot of hours. Saturdays. Saturday nights even."

He turned to see if there were any witnesses still around. Two kids and a guy who was probably a father were talking down the right field line.

"Lieutenant Schmidlin," I got out. "I'm sure you've met him?" He looked back at me and allowed me to continue. "I've met him too. Couple of times. Nice guy." I made him wait a few seconds. "Do you think he doesn't know you're selling drugs? On overtime I mean?"

I had him thinking. "What do you want?" he repeated.

"I want to know where your cousin is," I told him. "I feel I owe the kid."

He laughed a bit, but at the same time he looked like he wanted to pop me. "And with your keen private investigator mind you've somehow determined that I know where he is."

"Exactly," I said. "And you know I'm right, which is why you did that Neanderthal act on my car. A bit extreme for some petty drug sales, but for murder…"

"Murder?" He started to put a finger in my face, but then turned to see if the two kids and the dad were still there. They were slowly starting to walk away.

"Before you do yet another stupid thing, hear me out here," I said. "If I know about your drug deals, then obviously Schmidlin knows too, and if I know that you know what happened to your cousin, then obviously Schmidlin knows that too. So if something happens to me… well what would Bob think then?"

He had to work at not tearing me apart. "That kid's always been weird," he blurted out. "Always. He murdered my father. My *father!* I don't know where the little shit is and I couldn't care less." His jaw was trembling.

I looked him in the eye. "Then who knows?" I asked. "Who are you protecting?"

He started a little more friendly-like. "Look, Cello, I just lost my father. That's bad enough under any circumstances… but when the guy dies in a pool he's been swimming in for years… and then the State Police are all over the family when things are bad enough already…" He turned both palms upward. "I don't know where the kid is. I think he might have somehow… Maybe somehow he was responsible for my father. Like I said, he was always a little weird. To tell you the truth, I don't miss him. The only reason I'd want him found is so he could spend the rest of his miserable pathetic life in prison being somebody's girlfriend."

I studied him for a moment and then said, "Okay. Thanks." I removed a business card from my wallet and carefully stuffed it in his shirt pocket. "If you think of anything, I'd appreciate it if you'd let me know."

I turned to the side and started to walk away, but he called after me. "Hey, Cello."

I stopped and turned back toward him.

"If Schmidlin's so sure I'm… you know… the drugs… why doesn't he arrest me?"

"It's not like on TV," I told him. "If he bothers you repeatedly, you could charge him with harassment. But he thinks it's more than the drugs, so he's laying back and waiting."

"Waiting for what?" he asked.

"The mistake," I said. "Eventually, they always make a mistake."

He looked confused.

"Just my opinion," I told him. I turned again and this time I walked away.

A minute later, as I was driving off, I noticed that Tim Bradley had joined the three people standing by the foul line. He'd probably made note of what I was driving, but I figured he was more preoccupied with his computer at the pharmacy—how many grams of OxyContin or whatever.

It didn't make sense to go back into the city and then out again during the rush hour. I strolled the North Shore Mall, spending most of the time in a bookstore before having a combination plate at Peking Express in the food court. After a quick trip back to the car, I returned to the mall, went into the men's room, and changed into my Parents Club clothes—blue button-down oxford and navy blazer. I looked in the mirror and scared myself. Indeed, I could have been a dad.

The parking lot at St. Joseph's was pretty well packed. Several parents were still strolling from their vehicles to the front entrance of the two-story brick building.

Since Kevin was the only Bradley who hadn't yet met me, I figured it might be advantageous to resort back to my incognito thing and see what I could pick up. If that bore no fruit, I could always approach him as myself at the end of the evening.

The auditorium was about half full, with a lot of folks milling around talking. I felt I blended in nicely.

There was still five minutes to go before seven o'clock. I spotted a thirty-something dark-haired woman standing alone, smiling bravely at passers-by.

"Excuse me," I said. "This is my first meeting. I'm kind

of scouting the school out for next year. Are you pleased with it?"

"Oh, very much so," she said. She gave me a slightly confused look and then recovered and introduced herself. "Jessica Meuse," she informed me while extending a hand.

"Paul Scully. Nice to meet you."

Ms. Meuse smiled agreeably.

"So pardon my ignorance. What happens here? Does someone give a speech and then everybody has coffee?" I smiled and shrugged.

Jessica looked at me approvingly. "Well, more or less," she said. "Dr. Bradley, the president, starts it off by updating us with anything that's new, and then some of the Board members will contribute, and then there'll be an open dialogue with the parents." She laughed suddenly and lightly tapped me on the lapel. "And then we'll all drink coffee."

"Sounds like a fun evening," I said cheerfully. I looked toward the podium. "Which one is Dr. Bradley?"

She gave a single subtle nod in the general direction. "The gentleman there in the dark blue suit—tall, light hair."

"Looks like a nice enough guy," I said. "I'm going to mosey on over and see if I can work my way in. Thanks."

Jessica once again offered her brave little smile. I felt a tad guilty as I walked away.

Kevin Bradley was standing and chatting with two other men of roughly the same age. I casually worked my way behind him and pretended to look around the room while tuning into their conversation.

"So when are we taking it out?" I heard one ask jovially.

A third man walked passed me and joined them. The same guy who had just spoken spoke again. "Hey, Jack, Kevin bought a boat."

"All right!"

"Thirty foot Mintaka. I was just asking him when he's taking us out." They all laughed heartily.

"I'm going out on Wednesday," a new voice joined in. "Actually, I bought it two weeks ago, but with all that happened… Anyway, you're more than welcome to come along."

Somebody else started to say something, but another guy pointed out that it was time to start the meeting and I couldn't make out what the first guy said.

Kevin Bradley took his place at the podium, turned on the microphone, and began calling the meeting to order. As the crowd gradually grew silent, I made my way to the men's room and called directory assistance. There were three yacht clubs in the area—Palmer Cove, Devereux Beach, and Babson Point. I went back out, slid along the side, and took the first unoccupied end seat I came to.

Over the next forty-five minutes or so, the young Dr. Bradley, with the aid of his fellow board members, went through a list of items that included repairs in the rest rooms, a revised lunch menu, plans for the junior high's graduation, and a fund raiser for the new tennis courts. When it was over, he took a few questions from parents and then invited everybody to stay for coffee and cookies.

He was about twenty feet from the podium, talking to a couple of parents, when I moved in like a politician. Dismissing the parents with an insincere, "Excuse me," and leading with my extended hand, I gave an ostensibly heartfelt, "Dr. Bradley, I'm really sorry about your loss. I was out of town." I shook my head. "I'm really sorry."

Being both a local doctor and the President of the Parents Club, he couldn't admit that he didn't have a clue who I was. "Thank you," he said.

"Hey, I heard you bought a Mintaka," I said more enthusiastically. "Where are you docking her, Palmer, Devereux…?"

"Ah, Babson actually."

"Excellent!" I exclaimed while cuffing him on the shoulder.

"See you around the ocean." I pointed a finger at him and made a dynamic departure.

As soon as I got to the car, I called Peter at home. "Whatever you're doing on Wednesday, cancel it," I said. "We're going deep sea fishing."

The beautiful thing about Peter is that the more out of the blue and off the wall something is, the more it appeals to him. "Great!" he said. "I'll call Frank."

I explained to him that for me it was going to be more of an investigative mission that would take place at the yacht club. He wasn't the least bit dissuaded. If it was spontaneous and out of the ordinary, that's all he needed.

As I started the car to head back home, I began to think about pouring a couple of glasses of Chianti and sitting back with Nicole and Cedric to watch the Maine timber segment. I glanced over at my original change of clothes and my one-hundred-dollar candlestick holders. It had been a long day, but it was finally over. Or at least that was what I thought at the moment.

Chapter 13

Maybe I was getting paranoid or maybe it was just a coincidence, but the car behind me had taken every turn I had all the way out to Route 128. Of course 128 was a major highway; why shouldn't somebody else be heading out to it the same way I was?

I stayed all the way over on the right, and even though I didn't accelerate all the way up to normal highway speed, the other car stayed right behind me. When I saw an opening, I cut across two lanes, all the way to the left, and began passing cars in the center lane. My companion did the same. After passing two cars and an SUV, I signaled and moved over into the center lane, then decelerated enough so as not to leave room for anyone to squeeze in behind me. Instead of passing, he simply kept pace, about thirty feet off to the left of my rear bumper. I found little comfort in the reassurance that I was not becoming paranoid.

After cruising in the middle lane for several minutes with my uninvited guest still on my tail at seven o'clock, I signaled right and then moved over in that direction. The other car accelerated enough to get into the center lane, but immediately after he did so, I slowed on the right so as not to allow him to get in behind me. He would either have to pass, or ride right beside me. He chose the latter. I looked over expecting to see Tim Bradley's Saab, but instead it was a large dark sedan, probably green. I couldn't make out the model. The driver had what was probably a fishing hat pulled down on the near side and he was driving with his head turned a bit to the left. Whoever he was, he knew I was onto him.

Experience had taught me that once the subject was aware that he was being followed, it served little purpose to continue the pursuit. Eventually, he would stop somewhere, and at that point, the tail had only two options—he could either continue on by and concede defeat, or he could get out and be confronted by the subject. *The day will come when you'll wish you had one.* I told the little man to shut up so that I could think clearly.

A few minutes later, I started to gradually slow down. The green sedan beside me did the same. The driver behind me finally lost his patience and went around both of us. As soon as that maneuver had been completed, the guy in the sedan hit the brakes and then moved quickly into the vacated space behind me. He was determined not to let me get behind him and escape at the next exit.

I would have been able to read the number off his license plate into the memo recorder, but he didn't have a front plate.

At the junction of Route 1, I merged heading south toward the city, and of course it was no surprise when my tail did the same.

For the next few miles, I continued to head home while weighing my options. Obviously, whoever did the job on the Z4 already knew where I lived, so there was nothing to lose by simply going home. But I was getting irritated. Who was this joker? As I approached the incline to the Northeast expressway, I decided I'd pull over in the lighted parking lot of the next plaza. Presumably, he would at least have a license plate in the rear. I'd either get the number or, if he too stopped, I'd walk over and find out what it was that he wanted with me. I might have been encouraged by the fact that I'd already escaped death once that day.

But then something totally unexpected happened. As I started up the ramp to the expressway, he turned off to the right into Revere.

The only thing I could think of was that he was satisfied that I was going home. Instead of being relieved, though, I found myself feeling disappointed. I didn't have the registration, the make of the car, or a description of the driver. But I also knew that I had probably not seen the last of him.

The rest of Monday night went pretty much as planned. I'd called Nicole from the car and she had the popcorn ready when I got in. After an extra energetic greeting from Cedric, the three of us settled in and watched the Maine timber segment. I once again marveled at Ms. Doucette doing her usual fine job of opening people up. It seemed to come natural, probably because she was so honest herself. But I didn't let on that I was left less optimistic than she about the fate of many of those poor people.

At breakfast on Tuesday morning, Nicole told me about Dan-the-anchorman's family vacation and a segment she was going to be doing on Portuguese eateries in New Bedford. I filled her in on Tim Bradley, and told her about the hundred-dollar candlestick holders I was now the proud owner of. I didn't mention that I'd once again been followed.

As usual, when Nicole went off to work, I read the sports page over a second cup of coffee before heading out the door.

My destination was the Perrin Art Gallery. I was curious about the blue car that often took Jill Bradley away for four hours at a time. Of course now that husband Tim had seen the Volvo, I couldn't effectively use that, and since the night before I'd also been tailed in that car, I didn't want to swap cars with Nicole and needlessly endanger her. I had to rent something.

A dark-colored SUV would suit my purpose. The high driving position was always advantageous for tailing someone. After being on the wrong end of that experience on two of the past three days, I felt I was entitled.

As usual, I removed my Red Sox cap and sunglasses from

the glove compartment before leaving my own car in the parking lot of a shopping plaza. The rental place was just a five-minute walk up Route 1.

The black Nissan Pathfinder would do nicely. I placed the sunglasses inside the hat, tossed them on the shotgun seat, and headed east toward the coast.

The dashboard clock said 11:36 when I pulled into a parking space beyond the Perrin Gallery, facing Route 127. Newspaper at the ready, I sat and waited.

At 12:02 a blue Mazda sedan approached from 127, then turned and disappeared into the little parking lot. I raised the paper in front of my face and, with one eye, looked through the pinhole I'd poked in the back page. The car reappeared nose end out as Jill Bradley was locking the door to her shop. After she had walked over and gotten in, the blue sedan headed back out toward 127.

Adorned in baseball cap and sunglasses, I dropped the paper onto the seat and took off in subtle pursuit. They turned right onto 127 heading south. I intentionally let one other car get in between at the corner. Less than ten minutes later, after crossing into Gloucester, they turned left and headed toward the Point. Right behind them now, I read the plate number into the memo recorder and tried to lie back as much as possible. Another left onto a residential street. If they were watching, this could tip them off, but I had to go for it. Three quarters of the way down the block, they pulled into a driveway. I made a mental note of the blue cedar-shingled saltbox and continued on by, looking straight ahead as I did so.

Just before tuning left at the end of the street, I caught them in the side mirror, walking toward the house. I drove down to the next street, turned around, and took my time coming back. When I turned the corner again, they were out of sight, presumably in the house. I parked on the right side, still about five houses away. If it was what it appeared to be, I'd be there for another three and a half hours.

The ocean wasn't far behind me; I could smell the salt water and hear the gulls. That's nice for about ten minutes. I convinced myself that it was nothing more than the obvious and decided I'd give it exactly one hour total.

At precisely 1:25, I turned the key to the ignition and abandoned the mission. I could always come back later; it was unlikely that anything would have changed.

I took the highway back south into Lynnfield and parked across the street and a few doors over from the Garden Club. Again donned in cap and sunglasses, I watched and waited for the meeting to end, hoping I'd see Ellen Bradley, although I wasn't sure exactly why I wanted to.

Less than a half-hour had passed when the door of the white stucco building opened and people, mostly middle-aged women, started to emerge. First one car and then a second pulled up and double-parked right out in front. Once again making use of the newspaper, I spotted Ellen Bradley descending the stairs. She stopped at the bottom, chatted with another woman on the sidewalk for a moment, and then got into the second of the two cars that were double-parked. I turned the ignition and got ready to roll.

As the black Mercedes slowly pulled away, I got close enough to read yet another plate—only four numbers. They drove out to Route 1, headed south for a mile or so, and then pulled into the parking lot of the Hillside restaurant.

Satisfied that they were going in for a late lunch, I drove past, reversed direction at the next exit, and headed back north toward Gloucester. On the way, I pulled Peter up on his cell.

"You at the station?"

"Yeah, some guy lost his goldfish, but then his cat called and said he had it, but then—"

"I need you to run a couple of plates for me."

I waited while he went through his obligatory protest. When he was finished, I gave him the numbers. He pretended not to have written them down. I thanked him and told him I'd call back in an hour.

It was early enough that I had time to take a spin by the gallery to make sure it was still closed. It was. Back to Gloucester.

The blue Mazda was still parked in the driveway and the same parking space was still available down the street. If the antique dealer was right, they wouldn't come out for another half-hour.

It was a bit early, but I called Peter.

"Hey I heard back from Frank," he said, excitedly. "We're on for tomorrow."

"Great. I'll call you tonight and we'll finalize the plans. Any luck with those numbers?"

"Yeah, I've got them right here..." His voice trailed off for a moment as he turned away from the phone. "Blue Mazda?"

"That's one of them."

"David Gamser, Gloucester. And the other one I remember was a Mercedes... Wait, I've got it right here." I could hear papers rustling. "It belongs to a... hold on a minute... Dr. Harold Golden."

I got both addresses—the one I was at and the other one, in Saugus.

Now I at least had something to think about while I waited for the lovers to emerge. I remembered the photo in the library. My imagination ran wild with all kinds of possibilities. It was almost a distraction when Jill Bradley and David Gamser finally came out of the house and climbed back into the blue Mazda.

Lying back as much as possible, I carefully followed them north into Rockport. When the Mazda turned down the street where the gallery was, I drove on by, turned onto the next street, circled the block, and approached the gallery from the opposite direction. I was just in time to see Jill Bradley reopening her gallery door as the blue sedan escaped up the street. Presumably, she drove to work in her own car everyday. Why did she have to get picked up and delivered?

Just before merging onto 128, I called directory assistance for Saugus, Massachusetts. If all Ellen Bradley and Dr. Golden did was have an early dinner, the doctor should be home by now. Of course that wasn't what I actually expected, so I was surprised when a man answered. After confirming that it was in fact Dr. Golden I was speaking to, I genially engaged him.

"I apologize for calling you at home, doctor. My name is Dean Cello. I'm investigating the unfortunate death of your friend Dr. Bradley. I wonder if you would be so kind as to grant me a small piece of your time, sir?"

"I've heard about you, Mr. Cello." He sounded relaxed. "I tell you what. I was just about to pour myself a glass of port. Why don't you come over and join me?"

If it showed that I'd been caught off guard, the doctor didn't let on. I told him I could be at his house within the hour and he graciously said he was looking forward to meeting me.

After calling Nicole to let her know I'd be late again, I returned the rented SUV, and then headed straight for the home of Dr. Harold Golden.

The house was a mostly brick structure, not all that common in the area. As might be expected, the grounds were meticulously maintained—lush lawn with islands featuring mostly rhododendrons. A weeping cherry tree was just a couple of days away from erupting into full bloom.

The doctor greeted me with a warm smile. "There's the man I've been hearing about." His handshake, like that of his old friend, was firm but not overbearing. And also like his old friend, he led me to a study. Through a pair of French doors at the back, I could see a brick walkway that gave the appearance of winding off into the woods.

He handed me the port. "Ellen told me about you," he acknowledged as he motioned for me to sit in one of the burgundy wing chairs adjacent to a wall of books. "She likes you. Says you were brought up properly." His broad smile betrayed the fact that he found the observation somewhat amusing. As I looked back at him, I decided the picture in the library hadn't done him justice. He was a large, handsome man—the type that might actually look better bald.

"That's certainly very kind of her," I offered.

"It's never a matter of kindness with Ellen," he lightheartedly commented. "She calls 'em as she sees 'em." I was still trying to figure out how to respond to that when he asked, "So what can I do for you, Mr. Cello?"

"Dean, if you don't mind."

He nodded his agreement. "And I'm Howard."

I nodded too. "Well, I suppose you know I'm a private investigator and I'm investigating Dr. Bradley's death," I started. "I'm aware that that might sound odd, even audacious maybe. I mean with the police being involved and all."

"And with you doing it unsolicited and free of charge," he added amusedly.

I looked back at him. "Yeah, that too," I conceded.

His expression seemed more one of guarded admiration than condescension. He needed to hear more.

"I don't know how much Mrs. Bradley told you…"

"Start at the beginning, Dean. I've got another bottle where this one came from."

Despite that proclamation, I had noticed that he'd thus far taken only one small sip. Maybe it was the company he was craving. "Do you live alone?" I heard myself ask.

"Since Martha died," he said, his smile waning only slightly. "It'll be five years in August."

"I'm sorry."

He nodded again.

In deference to his request, I started at the beginning—Dr. Bradley's phone call, my meeting with Brian, the news of the doctor's death. I paused and thought for a moment before deciding to go for it.

"Doctor… Howard, there's something that I thought odd at the time, and now, even though I've met and very much enjoyed the company of Mrs. Bradley… well on the Sunday morning after the incident, I called the doctor's house to ask him if I could drop by to return his check and Mrs. Bradley said… her exact words were, 'You shan't have to do that. You see, Mr. Cello, the doctor is dead.'"

Golden slapped his thigh and roared with laughter. All I could do was watch him and wait. Eventually, he got to me and I emitted a small chuckle of my own. When he finally got past it, he explained.

"That's Ellen alright. I told you she calls 'em as she sees 'em." He leaned his large frame forward and rested his forearms on his knees. Speaking more seriously, he began to explain. "I've known Ellen Bradley for years. When Martha was alive, the four of us did everything together. Golf, bridge, vacations… everything. At first blush you might think Ellen is either shallow or frightened, or maybe both—hiding from reality behind some pretentious facade. But let me tell you something. That woman is no dummy. She held that family together. And it was no easy task either."

When he paused, I remained silent. He studied me for a moment and then decided to continue.

"When Connor's sister died… Brian's mother… Connor and Ellen took the boy in. He was only ten years old then. His father hadn't been around for years. Arizona, last anyone heard. Anyway, Brian's entrance into the family when Kevin and Tim were still teenagers themselves… well it wasn't that they were cruel to him or anything like that, but Kevin and Tim had always been very close to their father and suddenly…

suddenly the family dynamics were changed overnight. There were times when one boy or the other felt Connor was paying too much attention to Brian. They were used to having their dad all to themselves—golf, sailing, ballgames. Even during the teenage years they'd remained close. And Connor… well obviously Connor never meant to turn his back on his own boys, but he knew his nephew needed special attention. Hell, the kid had been abandoned by his father and then when his mother… Plus he wasn't the biggest kid in the schoolyard; you know how it is. Anyway, Connor spent a lot of time with the kid, trying to build his self-confidence."

By the time he paused to take a sip of his port, I was wondering enough that I had to ask. "And Ellen? How was it that she held the family together?"

"Ellen was the glue," he said, not hiding his admiration. "Ellen had a way with both her husband *and* her sons. Usually she was so subtle that they never even knew she was working them."

"And how about Brian? How did Ellen and Brian relate?"

"She never reached the point with Brian that she reached with her own sons," he admitted. "I remember once when the four of us were out to dinner, she confided that she felt herself holding back. Said she didn't want the boy to think she was being presumptuous, that she realized she could never take the place of his own mother."

I nodded my understanding and took a sip of wine. My host did the same.

"But it wasn't all Brian," he continued. "By the time the boys were going off to college… Well actually it wasn't so much Kevin; things always seemed to come pretty easy to him, but Tim… Tim had always tried so hard to please his dad. For one thing, though, he was never as bright as Kevin. And even though Connor gave him every bit as much attention as he gave Kevin, Tim somehow always seemed to feel he was living in his brother's shadow. Then, even though they were older and already out of the house... I think when Tim couldn't make it through medical school... The poor guy studied twice as hard as his brother, but he just couldn't do it. Finally had to give up. Not that pharmacology isn't an honorable profession. And of course Connor gave him most of the down payment on the pharmacy, which in retrospect was probably a mixed blessing."

"Why a mixed blessing?"

"Well there you have Kevin making it on his own, eventually even going into business with his father, and Tim needs help to buy second best. And then of course there was that business with his wife."

He had trailed off on that last sentence and I almost didn't want to ask, but of course I had to.

"Business with his wife?"

Dr. Golden looked as though he regretted having mentioned it. He seemed to size me up again and then apparently decided I was worthy.

"Just about this time last year, she attempted suicide. Sleeping pills."

He didn't want to elaborate any more and I didn't want to push it.

Dr. Golden finished off his port and poured himself another. I told him I was fine.

"How about Tim and Brian?" I asked. "How did they get along?"

"It was cordial only until about a year ago. It seems Tim has taken an interest in Brian's music. He goes to listen to the band a lot."

Dr. Golden stopped. It seemed he'd said about all he had to say about the Bradley family history. But there was still something nagging at me.

"Awhile ago, and I know this is probably silly... When I told you about Ellen saying 'The doctor is dead,' you found that rather amusing. Forgive me, but the humor escapes me."

He smiled warmly and again nodded his understanding. "Ellen has that reserved, proper way about her. Then when you least expect it, she hits you with something like that, right between the eyes. I guess it's the sudden contrast that always strikes me as amusing."

"Again, forgive me, but her husband of three decades had just died."

"Mm, I can see how you'd think it was strange. But that's what I was telling you about before. You think she's weak, but she's anything but. She goes on about etiquette on all, but down inside she knows that life has its cruel side and she's ready for it. She won't run and hide. She'll stand up to whatever the reality is and look it straight in the eye. It sounds to me as though you caught her at such a moment. She wouldn't delude her self with "passed away" or "deceased." Not at that moment, anyway. You obviously spoke to her just as she was facing the horrible reality straight on. I imagine she said it for herself more than for you. You just happened to be there to hear it." His admiration appeared to have no boundaries.

"You obviously think a great deal of Ellen Bradley."

"I do. As I said, the four of us were very close. And now there's only two of us left." The big man's eyes moistened. I rose from my seat.

"Thank you very much for your time, Doctor."

"Howard," he corrected me. "And you're quite welcome."

I saved the big question for the door. "Howard, what do you think happened to Connor?"

"I don't know," he conceded. He seemed visibly shaken.

I just stood there and looked back at him for a pregnant moment.

"But I'm not sure it was an accident," he finally added.

What did I have to lose? "Indulge me," I implored with a friendly smile. "Where were you between seven and nine P.M. on that Saturday night?"

If he was offended, he didn't show it. "I was at my sister's house," he said. "In Topsfield. The police have already checked it out."

I thanked him again and walked out into the dusk.

As I started the car I realized that more than ever I had more questions than answers. That was okay though. In fact experience had taught me that that was usually a good thing. At least now I had specific questions.

Driving back toward Boston, I continued to think about the Bradley family, adding all that Dr. Golden had said into the equation. I remembered that when I first read about them in the *The Villager*, I thought they were all so squeaky clean. Now I had a son illicitly selling drugs, a suicidal daughter-in-law screwing around with whomever, a best friend probably putting the moves on the wife while her husband's body was still warm, and another daughter-in-law wanting to screw around with *me*. Squeaky clean my ass.

That last thought reminded me of something I was supposed to do. Peter answered on the first ring.

"Hey, before we get into the plans for tomorrow," I said, "I need to ask a couple of technical questions to a forensic psychiatrist. You guys must contract with one, right?"

"Sure. Dr. Meier. He likes me. For just a couple of questions, I can set you up for free. He's a wine aficionado, so just be sure to bring him something expensive."

Grateful, I didn't bother to point out the incongruity.

After we laid out the plan for the fishing expedition, Peter gave me a heads-up. "It's only fair that I warn you. Frank's ah… well he's bit out there. Be ready."

Peter warning me that somebody was "a bit out there." Tomorrow was going to be a keeper.

Chapter 14

I arrived at the Babson Point Yacht Club just after sunrise, attired in jeans, sweatshirt, fishing cap, and deck shoes. It was the first time in almost two years that I missed my early morning run and I was a bit distressed about it. After I was there for a couple of minutes, though, the gentle sloshing of the waves against the dock pilings and the calls of the gulls echoing across the bay seemed to have a soothing effect. Maybe I'd run further tomorrow.

I'd gone online to learn that a Mintaka was a single-mast sailboat, and one of Kevin Bradley's buddies had said it was a thirty-footer. Trouble was it seemed there were quite a few boats at Babson Point that fit that description. Not to worry though; I figured somebody would be awake early and it was likely that he or she would know the illustrious Kevin Bradley, doctor, Parent Club President, and general pillar of the community.

The first breathing soul I saw was a sandy-haired, forty-something guy with a couple of days' worth of whiskers. He had just emerged from his cabin and was running one hand through his hair while holding a cup of coffee in the other.

"Excuse me. I'm supposed to meet Dr. Kevin Bradley here and I don't remember which one he's at."

"Fourteen," he said agreeably. "Little early for Kevin, though."

"Yeah, I just wanted to make sure I knew where I was going. I'm gonna take a quick look at his new toy, then come back later. Thanks."

The unshaven guy hoisted his coffee at me and then looked out across the bay. I walked down five more boats and stood to admire the *Carol Ann*. Oak with black trim and a royal blue sail. It looked bigger than I'd expected.

When I felt I'd seen enough, I retraced my steps and then walked out onto an adjacent pier. I pulled up Peter on his cell.

"I'm at Babson Point. I found the boat."

"Great. I'm on my way to the Winthrop Marina now. I'm sure Frank's already there. He's really up for this. Last night he told me it'll be like he's back on the force again."

"How can I turn down another expert's offer to help? Look, I'll be in the restaurant, okay? It's the dark red building. How long do you figure it's going to take you to get here?"

"We'll be leaving here in five minutes. I figure about forty-five, an hour tops."

"That'll work out fine. Some guy I just talked to implied that my man isn't an early riser. We'll do breakfast and keep an eye out. In fact I'm going to go grab a cup of coffee and a window seat."

After disconnecting, I slid on my shades, readjusted the fishing hat, and walked up to the restaurant. Apparently I was the first customer. There didn't seem to be any waiters yet either. The cook was early forties, big arms, blue short sleeve jersey.

"Morning," he called over. "What can I get you?"

"Just coffee for now. I'm waiting for some friends."

I approached the counter as he poured my coffee. "Actually, I had two offers today and, as it turns out, the second one was better, but I'd already said yes to the first."

He placed the coffee down in front of me and looked across the counter. If I wanted to talk, he was willing to listen.

"A couple of friends asked me to go fishing and that seemed like a good idea until Kevin Bradley asked me to join him on his new toy."

The cook smiled agreeably. "Well it's going to be a great day weather wise. I'm sure you'll enjoy the fishing too."

"I'm sure I will," I conceded, and carefully took my first sip of the steaming coffee.

"Where do you know Dr. Bradley from?" he asked.

"Parents Club at Saint Joseph's in Danvers. And he's my doctor too. Well actually his father was my doctor, but…" I shook my head.

"Yeah, that was an awful thing," he agreed. "One of the nicest guys I've ever met."

I looked at him for a moment, and then speaking softly, pretended to confide. "Hey, I haven't actually had a conversation with Kevin about it yet and I don't want to say the wrong thing, but… I've heard the police are investigating the matter. Have you heard anything about that?"

He considered whether or not he wanted to go there, and then volunteered, "Everyone around here's betting on the nephew."

I looked confused. "The nephew. What nephew?"

"The one that lived with them for years." He tilted his head. "How well did you know Connor?"

"He was my doctor." I shrugged. "I've gotten to know Kevin much better. Mostly from the Parents Club."

The cook nodded and then took a sip from his mug. "When Connor's sister died years ago, that left the kid without a home. I wasn't here back then; I heard about it later. Anyway, apparently Connor took the kid in. Story goes that the kid was kind of timid. The doctor sort of made him a special project. Spent a lot of time with him." He paused suddenly and just looked at me.

"So if he was so nice to the kid, why would the kid want to…?" I tossed my head.

He decided he wasn't going to say any more. "Ask Kevin. I'm sure he'll tell you about it. And it'll be much more enjoyable while you're out there cutting through the water."

"Except that I'll be fishing," I reminded him.

"Oh, yeah," he acknowledged with a smile. But he wasn't

going to add anything else. He meandered down ten feet or so and stopped where his *Globe* was spread out on the counter. I noticed there was a stack of them by the register and it occurred to me that I hadn't seen the paper yet myself. After leaving two singles on the counter, I walked over and, paper in hand, claimed my window seat.

It seemed like only a half-hour had passed when I spotted a small white boat approaching the landing at high speed. As the two men slowed to tie up, I saw that it was indeed Peter and his future father-in-law. The latter wasn't a tall man, but he had a large frame and appeared to be quite fit. What hair remained was white, as was the mustache, which rivaled Peter's in thickness. I left the restaurant and walked down to the dock to greet them.

I looked at my watch. "See, you're early again," I pointed out.

Peter was grinning broadly. I got the impression that he had very much been looking forward to this meeting. His introduction, although succinct, was enthusiastic—"Dean Cello, Frank Capachietti." Then he just stood there and watched.

Frank extended his hand. "Hey, how's it goin', Dino?" The Italo-American accent was familiar to me from having grown up in the North End.

"Nice to meet you, Frank," I offered while shaking his hard hand.

He looked at Peter as he flipped a thumb toward me and paraphrased. "'Nice to meet you.' You're right; he is a fancy talker."

Frank cuffed me on the shoulder. "So what do we got here, Dino?" he asked.

I didn't know how to say it so I just came out with it. "If you don't mind, Frank, I prefer Dean."

He looked at me. He wasn't sure.

I couldn't help it; I laughed. "No, really," I said. "I mean it's not that I'm not proud of my heritage. I am. It's just that I like to think of myself as an American first. If you don't mind."

Frank raised both hands in surrender fashion. "Hey, you're you, huh? You want it to be Dean, you got it." Another shoulder cuff.

The three of us headed back to the restaurant where we ordered big breakfasts and I filled Frank Capachietti in on all that had happened thus far. When I finished, Frank looked over at me and then decided to finish off his last strip of bacon before responding.

"So this is a watch and see what happens operation," he more stated than asked.

"Basically, yeah. I know it's a long shot, but I've got at least a little something on everyone else in the family. I thought it was time I see what this guy's about—who his friends are. And there's always a chance we could pick up something in conversation around here." I realized that to a seasoned cop, that probably sounded ridiculous. "Besides, it's a nice day for a boat ride."

"I think you gotta make contact."

"Okay."

I waited, but he didn't elaborate.

"How?"

"Leave that up to Uncle Frank," he said.

Peter failed in a valiant attempt to suppress a laugh, and when I looked over at him, his hand was covering his mouth. His eyes, however, screamed borderline hysteria.

The cook came over and cleared our dishes. Apparently at this early hour he was the whole show, which seemed to make sense. Only one other table was occupied—two couples.

"You boys want some more coffee?"

It was Frank who answered immediately. "That'd be nice. Thank you."

The cook returned and refilled the three cups. He had just

turned to go back behind the counter when Frank unabashedly removed a little nip of Sambuca from his jacket pocket and poured half its contents into his coffee. "'Some 'buca, Dean?" He held what was left high up over the table.

"No thanks, Frank. It's a bit early for me."

"You and him," he said, motioning with his head toward Peter who was sitting next to him. "Like I've tried to explain to him, it ain't about the alcohol. It makes the freakin' coffee taste better."

While Frank was taking the first sip of his better-tasting coffee, I glanced out the window and saw someone who could have been Kevin Bradley with two other guys about the same age. All three were dressed in white shorts and jerseys. The one that could have been Kevin was carrying a windbreaker over his shoulder. The other two guys had theirs tied around their waists. None of them looked up at the restaurant. They headed straight down the pier to where the *Carol Ann* was docked.

Frank asked Peter if he'd seen the ballgame last night. Peter explained that he'd turned it on just in time to catch the error that had cost them the game.

"That's them," I interrupted, looking over my shoulder at the three guys boarding the *Carol Ann*.

Peter and Frank both looked out the window.

"Alright," Frank muttered as he nodded, a thin smile crossing his lips. "We still got time to finish our coffee. By the time they set the sails, a vast yee matees, and all that other freakin' sailin' stuff..."

We talked baseball for the next five minutes while Frank and Peter both kept an eye on the *Carol Ann*. The boat was to my back. Finally, Peter nudged Frank and said, "Let's go."

"Alright," Frank muttered again while still keeping his eyes focused on the trio. He finished off what was left of his coffee, left too much money on the table, signaled for neither one of us to challenge that breakfast was on him, and slid out of the seat.

We climbed aboard Frank's boat, a twenty-seven-foot Criss Craft. I hadn't been on a boat since my parents died. I'd sold my father's along with the place on Winnipesaukee.

We motored slowly past the *Carol Ann*, paying no apparent notice as we did so. Just three guys going fishing.

Once clear of the docks, Frank swung us around to the right behind a narrow strip of land, just out of sight. I had checked with Peter earlier to make sure he hadn't forgotten the field glasses. He hadn't.

A few minutes later the top of the royal blue sail appeared, making its way out into the harbor. We laid back and waited until it was a fair distance out to sea before heading out ourselves.

I felt discouraged. And stupid. I had hoped that Kevin Bradley might enter the restaurant, where I could have listened in on the conversation and possibly actually learned something. But it now appeared that he was going to sail and we were going to fish and the only possible opportunity for contact would be when everybody returned at the end of the day. *If* in fact Kevin and his buddies stopped for a drink or a bite to eat.

For some reason, though, Peter and Frank didn't seem to share my frustration. I figured they were already doing what they enjoyed doing anyway. Indeed they had locked their lines over the side and were already working on their second beers. The sun was getting hot; I decided to take off my sweatshirt and go for a beer myself. Shortly after that, I too dropped a line in the water. What else was there to do?

Over the next hour and a half or so, we talked sports, politics, and work. Frank seemed more interested than I would have expected concerning what it had been like to be a teacher.

"I always thought that had to one of toughest freakin' jobs in the world," he said. "I think back to how I must've driven my own teachers crazy. Did they deserve that?" He took the liberty of answering his own question. "Hell no they didn't. They were just doing their best to get somethin' through this thick skull of mine." After pondering a couple of seconds more, though, he let himself off the hook. "But I turned out okay in the end."

As it happened, I was the first to get a bite. Peter excitedly issued his instructions one after the other. "Keep the line tight. Don't let him throw the lure. Get the butt of the rod down between your legs. Pull back on the rod, then reel down."

"I *have* done this before," I reminded him.

"Yeah, and brontosauruses ate palm trees," he said.

But it all seemed to come back quite naturally, and a few minutes later I hauled in what was probably about an eight-pound bluefish. After carefully removing the hook from its mouth and dumping it into the fish box, I flashed my old friend a winning smile.

"Bullshit!" he protested. "That's only because Frank knew where to position the boat. If you were out here on your own, you'd starve to death."

Frank just looked at us and smiled knowingly. He'd undoubtedly witnessed many such exchanges in his time.

I picked up the field glasses and checked again to make sure the tiny sail in the distance to the northeast was indeed that of the *Carol Ann.* It was. I reached for another beer.

The boat bobbed gently in the water, the sun caressed our shoulders, and the cares of the world all seemed to have been left back on the land. Screw Kevin Bradley. I deserved a day off anyway.

Frank casually asked Peter what his schedule looked like for the rest of the week and Peter mentioned that he had promised Linda he would paint the foyer. He mockingly pronounced foyer with the French accent, which apparently prompted Frank to share a thought.

"French," he said. "What kind of a language is that? They don't pronounce half the letters. So what are they there for?"

A few minutes later, Frank pulled in a blue. It was just a little smaller than the one I'd already caught. That left Peter the only one without a fish so far. I smiled at him again.

Not long after that, I hauled in another one. After putting it in the box, I told Peter, "Don't worry, pal. I'm sure you'll get one before the day is out."

The three of us fished in silence for a while, and then Peter shared with us the details of a drug case he was working on.

"Kids today," Frank said, shaking his head. "We used to think we were doin' somethin' when we stole an apple from Judge Landry's yard. Now you gotta do crack." He shook his head again. "God bless you guys that'll be bringin' up kids these freakin' days."

He didn't express the thought cavalierly; he really seemed to care. I got the impression that Frank was one those people who got increasingly mellow as he became inebriated.

It was probably a combination of things that caused me to ask. I was working on my fourth beer, Frank seemed a lot more real than he had been at first, and I'd just heard "freakin'" for about the fiftieth time.

"Hey, Frank, can I ask you something?"

He turned to look at me. "Ask away," he said.

"How come you say 'freakin' so much?"

The question had just come out of my mouth when Peter announced, "I got to hit the head," and disappeared into the cabin.

Frank finished off his beer before turning to answer me.

"My wife," he said. "My Mary, she was a saint. She hated when I used the F word. So when she… at her wake, I was kneeling down at the casket and I made her a promise. I said,

'Mary, I want you to be proud of me. And so I'm never gonna use that word for the rest of my life. Ever. I'm doin' this for you, Mary. Because I know it'll make you happy.' That's what I said. So after that I got in the habit of usin' 'freakin.' As a substitute, you know?" He tilted his head sideways and seemed to consider the idea anew. "It ain't so bad once you get used to it."

Frank looked at me amusedly. "So maybe I ain't so bad, huh?" he said. "Let me tell you somethin'. You guys got your college educations, and that's a good thing. But there's some things you learn just by bein' alive longer, you know what I mean? One of those things I've learned is this: Most people aren't on the outside who they really are on the inside, you know? I think on the outside you tend to act the way people acted where you were brought up. But over the years, things change on the inside. You get, ah... wiser, you know? And maybe that makes you change the way you act on the outside a little, but not that much I think. I think for the most part you still keep that other guy around, even though on the inside he died a long time ago. I don't know why, but that's the way it is."

I found myself nodding my understanding at him. "You must really miss her," I said.

"Yeah, I do," he said. He looked out at the ocean. "But you know, life is still worth livin'. I mean I still got Linda and Donna and fishin' and sunsets, you know? And people! Hey, people are always interestin'. So I figure no matter what, life is always worth livin'." He turned back toward me. "Hey, I know I'm gettin' old," he said. "And in the end I ain't gonna win the final decision. I'm just lookin' to pick up an occasional round here and there."

I looked back at him and nodded my admiration.

That won me another cuff on the shoulder. This time he tried to shake me a couple of times before letting go.

Less than five minutes after Peter came back topside, he pulled in his first bluefish. It was bigger than either of mine and it was bigger than Frank's. He proudly hung it by the gills for me to inspect.

I looked at Frank. "About nine pounds, wouldn't you say?"

"'Bout that," Frank said.

I looked up at the sky, thinking hard. "Let's see then. Eight and seven is fifteen… Fifteen to nine. Or two to one. Take your pick."

Peter laughed. He had his fish.

Frank grinned and said, "Okay, now we got some work to do, huh?"

He hit the throttle and turned the boat toward the northeast. "Which one of those sails is our guy?" he asked.

I wasn't sure. I needed the field glasses.

"The second from the right," I told him.

Peter reached for another beer. Frank held at a moderate speed and headed straight toward the target.

There was something about the look on Frank's face. A barely discernable knowing grin. He seemed to be rejuvenated. I decided not to ask.

Five minutes later, we were on a course to pass just in front of the *Carol Ann,* which was now only a few hundred feet away. Frank reduced our speed to under twenty knots, and immediately after having done so, let go of the wheel and reached for another beer. Then, seemingly out of nowhere, he started laughing with great gusto. He opened the beer and hoisted it high over his head, yucking it up as he did so. Peter then raised his beer and did the same.

I looked at the two of them. Then I looked at the *Carol Ann.* We were heading straight toward her starboard beam like a perfectly placed torpedo!

Frank nudged me with the back of his wrist. "Ain't that

funny!" he said, obviously trying to get me to join in. The two of them roared, paying no attention to the vessel they were about to broadside in fifteen seconds.

My first thought was I'd be damned if I was going to laugh at nothing just because two psychotics wanted to make it a trio. But then suddenly, as I watched them, I had an epiphany. Frank was over sixty years old. He had brought up children, mowed a lawn, and he still loved his departed wife. And he was *still crazy!* Nothing was going to change. My old pal Peter was going to be a goofy bastard forever! I let out a loud howl of rejoicing, and as I did so, I noticed that two guys on the deck of the *Carol Ann* were waving frantically and they appeared to be shouting at us. Kevin Bradley was at the wheel cutting it hard to port and looking over his right shoulder, eyes wide. Of course with all three of us laughing, we couldn't hear the guys yelling at us. Then, just when I thought we actually *were* going to broadside them, Frank appeared to miraculously notice them with a demonstrative startle. Throwing his beer overboard, he dove for the wheel and turned it just in time to barely graze the *Carol Ann.*

Frank immediately turned off the engine and the mood changed dramatically. In the relative silence, he offered an impassioned plea to the three men aboard the sloop.

"Aw, geesh, look at that," he said, extending an arm toward the scuff of white paint on the side of Dr. Kevin Bradley's brand new and expensive toy. "I'm so… Geez, I'm so sorry. But, hey, they can get that out, you know."

The young doctor was scarlet. He stood at the rail, speechless, arms wide. "You… You…" After a couple of false starts, he finally got it together. "What were you doing? What were you thinking?"

Frank looked confused. "Which one?" he wanted to know.

Kevin Bradley blinked and shook his head several times before silently throwing his hands up in disbelief.

"Hey, I really am sorry," Frank tried again. "Of course, I'm gonna take care of this. Come on. Let us up there and we'll do the right thing here. I'll make it good as new for you."

Kevin Bradley seemed not to have heard. He had turned toward me with narrowed eyes while slowly raising an accusatory finger. "I know you from somewhere," he said.

"I'm sure you don't, sir," I sung in my best southern accent. "I'm not from around here. Just visiting."

"No. NO!" he shouted, eyes wide and still pointing. "You're that guy at the Parents Club meeting." His hand was shaking violently. "You're that guy… I knew I didn't know you!"

"I'm afraid I don't know what you're talking about, sir."

"Hey," Frank interjected, looking up at Bradley. "Whatever. I'd just like to make arrangements to pay for the damage I inflicted on your boat, huh? Can we do that? Then we'll be on our way, huh? I promise we won't crash into you again." He shrugged and threw both palms up in front of his chest.

Eventually Kevin Bradley calmed down enough to allow Frank to hand over his address and phone number. The doctor did the same.

"You got the number on my boat," Frank said. "And you know where to find me, huh? Hey, again, I'm really sorry."

Just when things had gotten down to a reasonably civil level, I saw Peter suddenly lurch forward, eyes bulging. If everybody else had missed that spastic motion, they certainly couldn't miss the long howl that followed. And then the series of cackles. Tears streamed down his face as he sat doubled over. Dr. Bradley and his friends just stared in awe as Frank started the engine of the Criss Craft and slowly began to pull away.

Peter was still bent over when we were about a hundred feet away.

"What?" I asked.

It took him awhile to get it out, but between gasps he finally managed, "I just remembered that his wife wants to sleep with you."

"I freakin' love life," said Frank.

Chapter 15

My car was still parked at Babson Point, so Frank and Peter had to take me back there before making the return trip to Winthrop by sea. Once there, though, they joined me in the restaurant for a mid-afternoon meal consisting of steamers, quahogs, onion rings, and fries. Like three high school kids, we couldn't help reliving our not-so-chance encounter with Kevin Bradley. When I commented that it was a good time even if I didn't make any progress on the case, Frank, not surprisingly, offered some sage advice—"Fun is important too. Make progress tomorrow."

Before leaving Babson Point, I called Nicole and told her I'd bring her home a clam plate, which I knew she'd enjoy.

Finally, a relaxing evening with my woman and my dog. We played ball on the Common, then returned home where I watched the ballgame while Nicole did some research at the computer and then started browsing through a book about the history of New Bedford. In the morning she'd be leaving for a two-day tour of the Portuguese eateries.

On Thursday morning, I woke up even earlier than usual, so I made the most of it by running an hour ahead of schedule. As had become the norm now, Cedric joined me and didn't seem to notice that we were at it a bit earlier than usual. The rising sun shimmered orange off the Charles, and all indications pointed to another seasonably pleasant day.

When I emerged from the shower, Nicole was at the stove, piling up a stack of pancakes. I threw on jeans and a jersey and sat down at the table.

"Aren't we getting domestic," I said.

"I figured it was the least I could do. I'm leaving for New Bedford this morning, remember?"

"How could I forget that you're abandoning me again?"

"Cedric, bite him."

Cedric looked at me and tilted his head.

Since the New Bedford excursion was going to be a two-day affair, I wouldn't see Nicole again until Friday night.

An hour later I was in the recliner with my coffee and the sports page when she came back down to bid me good-bye.

"I'm off. Be careful. And remember, I won't be around to bail you out."

I got up to give her a hug. "Enjoy your linguica."

After Nicole left, I placed the paper down on the table lamp and again started mulling over the Bradley case. Certainly Kevin must have figured out who I was by now. If not after I left him at the Parents Club, then definitely after the incident on the high seas.

As I updated my notes, I considered that Kevin was still the one I knew the least about. That was probably okay, though. I heard in my head words Frank had uttered over dinner yesterday afternoon—"You never know, but if I had to bet, he's no killer." I realized that I too had held that opinion all along. In most cases, murder is in one way or another an act of desperation, and Kevin Bradley simply had too much going for him.

The computer clock said 9:27. I had an hour to go yet before my ten-thirty appointment with Dr. Benjamin Meier, consulting psychiatrist for the BPD.

I had just shut down when the phone rang. It was Nicole.

"Dean, turn on the news."

She didn't want to elaborate. I disconnected and did as she advised.

I figured it wasn't the five-day forecast or the commercial

for dishwasher detergent or the Sox edging out the Tigers, but when the next item appeared, it left no doubt.

"A grim discovery in Danvers early this morning. The body of a man thought to be in his early twenties was found in a wooded area..." The report went on to say that the young man was clothed in jeans and a sweatshirt and that preliminary reports seemed to indicate that he had been there for close to two weeks. A sunrise jogger and his dog had made the discovery. As disturbing as all that was, what was most troubling was the apparent cause of death—his head had been bashed in. Police had located a bloody sidewalk brick not far from where the body had been found. Forensic tests were being conducted.

If the police knew who the victim was, they hadn't released the name yet, but there was little doubt in my mind. It all fit too perfectly.

Before heading out the door, I gave Cedric a biscuit and a scratch. Cedric. I loved the beast, but under the circumstances, it was hard to rejoice at the thought that I might now get to keep him. Maybe.

Dr. Benjamin Meier's office was on the tenth floor of a high-rise on Atlantic Ave. I arrived promptly, a bottle of '97 Georges De LaTour Cabernet Sauvignon in hand.

The doctor was an average-sized man in his mid-forties, gray suit, thinning dark hair. He shook with his right hand while taking the bottle of wine with his left.

"Dean Cello, friend of the illustrious Sergeant Peter Perry," he bellowed cheerfully.

I couldn't resist. "Have you ever analyzed *him*, doctor?"

"I've given up on Sergeant Perry," he responded quickly. He was smiling as though he'd intended to be facetious, but I wondered. He motioned for me to have a seat in one of the club chairs in front of his desk. "So how can I help you?" he asked, taking his seat and clasping his hands beneath his chest.

"Well I have essentially two questions," I said. "Both involve an individual's potential for murder. I understand that you're a forensic expert, is that right?"

Without turning around, the doctor extended an arm toward the three diplomas hanging on the wall behind his desk. Then he opened a draw and silently passed his CV across to me. I didn't bother to examine it.

"Well," I started, "my first question is this: Is a person who has in the past been suicidal likely to somehow become *hom*icidal?"

Dr. Meier grinned. "Mr. Cello, in my profession anything is possible," he said. "But I'd have to say that the scenario you propose is highly unlikely. Suicidal individuals generally blame themselves for their troubles. While they may see themselves as victims, they hold out no hope for a constructive solution, and consequently, there appears to be nothing left worth living for. Conversely, while the homicidal individual might also see himself or herself as a victim, the self-preservation instinct remains intact, albeit in a perverted sort of way. When a homicidal person commits his act, he is, in effect, making an effort to right the perceived wrong and get on with his life."

Although I hadn't intended to speak yet, he held up a wait-a-minute finger before continuing.

"Of course this is all very general. There are probably as many possible scenarios as there are stars in the sky," he cautioned.

I wasn't trying to be a smart ass; I just kind of thought out loud. "So what you're saying is 'maybe.'"

"I live in a world of maybes," he said with a smile that came just short of a laugh. "The maybes become yeses or noes as I gradually learn more about the patient. Right now you're asking me to solve a ten factor equation when I have only one of the factors."

I nodded my understanding. "But basically it's *usually* the case that a suicidal person would not become homicidal. Is that right?"

"Usually," he succinctly conceded.

I took a deep breath. "Okay then. That leaves me with the other question. Could a son who's always felt inferior to his older brother be motivated to kill his own father?"

Dr. Meier smiled again and turned his palms up. "Again, anything is possible. But absent some truly abusive behavior on the part of the parent, I'd consider it highly unlikely."

"Well actually, I can be a bit more specific on this one," I said. "What I have is a son who has tried all his life to please his father, but has, not for want of trying, failed miserably. And while the father has probably never actually told the son that he is disappointed in him, the other son, two years older, has always done everything right. In fact, just recently, he inherited the father's medical practice."

"Possible, but not likely," he said.

We stared at one another for a moment before he finally decided to elaborate. "The scenario you describe actually plays out fairly frequently in one form or another. But absent blatant abuse on the part of the parent, the likelihood that someone would be driven to patricide would remain quite remote. In fact, the more typical syndrome would involve *self*-destructive behavior—alcoholism, drug abuse, inability to hold a job…"

O for 2. "Well, I guess you've told me what I wanted to know," I said, coming to my feet.

I reached across the desk and Dr. Meier stood to shake my hand again.

"Any time," he offered cheerfully. "And maybe next time, a nice Merlot."

I couldn't help but return his smile.

Since crossing downtown and finding a parking space along Atlantic Ave. would have been more trouble than it was worth, I'd simply walked to Dr. Meier's office. That meant

I now had about half an hour to think while walking back home.

If Tim and Jill were now long shots, that left Kevin, Carol, Ellen, and Dr. Golden. I'd just a couple of hours ago reiterated my conviction that Kevin was a highly unlikely possibility. Of the three suspects remaining, Carol seemed the most innocuous, so that left the wife and her friend good old Dr. Golden. Ironically, though, they were the two individuals who had thus far volunteered the most information. But of course I hadn't had any way to verify what they'd told me. Besides, even if they were responsible for Connor, why would they want to get rid of Brian? The most obvious answer to that was that Brian knew something. In fact what Brian might have known was simply that they were an item. And Brian was very close to his uncle. But if Brian knew something, anything, then why wouldn't he have told me about it that morning at Lou's Donut Shop?

I considered what might have been the two earlier attempts on Connor Bradley's life. The ones I originally scoffed at. Surely it couldn't be Ellen acting alone. The thought of her climbing up onto the roof to stuff a chimney was laughable, and the image of her rolling a fifty-two pound boulder off the overpass was something they hadn't yet invented a word for. Of course, as unlikely as it seemed, Dr. Golden could have done both. But on the night of the boulder incident, Connor Bradley had just left Golden's house. Golden would have to have taken an alternate route and arrived at the overpass well ahead of Connor. And along with the questions of Golden hiding the Mercedes and having the boulder ready, why would Connor take a less direct route home from a Friday night card game?

I looked up and noticed that I had walked through the financial district, turned left onto Tremont Street, and started into the Common without having seen any of it. But I now knew what I was going to do. I would pay another visit to the one person who was immediately accessible, to see what else I could learn, and then, later, I'd tail the other two.

I arrived at the bookstore shortly after noon. The bell chimed as I entered; Carol Bradley was working behind the counter. I had my PI license ready when she turned to face me.

"Dean Cello. I'm a private investigator. And I guess I owe you an apology," I offered contritely.

"I put two and two together," she said agreeably enough. "How was the fishing yesterday?" She started to laugh.

I'd forgotten how extremely attractive she was. "I'm so glad you're not angry with me," I said. "Look, if you wouldn't mind, I was hoping you could help me out with my investigation into the death of your father-in-law. I know I deceived you last week, but…"

"Besides Kevin, Connor was the only one I was close to. He was a kind and caring man. Whatever you need."

I was about to thank her when she suggested, "Let's go to lunch."

She reached under the counter and came up with one of those "We'll be back at…" signs. She fixed the hands on the cardboard clock to read 1:30, smiled at me, and snatched up her handbag on the way out from behind the counter. I turned to see that there were no customers present for her to be concerned about.

"I couldn't find a parking space," I told her. "I had to leave it way over on Summer Street. Mind if we take yours?"

The suggestion seemed to alarm her. "No," she quickly responded as she stopped suddenly and turned to face me. Then as she started out the door again, she laughed a bit and explained. "I mean if I leave my space I'll end up over on Summer Street myself. It happens every Thursday—street cleaning day on the other side of the square. Spaces are at a premium."

"Okay," I agreed. "As long as you don't mind walking all the way over to mine."

"Actually, we can just walk over to the Colonial Grill," she suggested. "They make an excellent steak sandwich. As long as you don't mind casual."

"Love casual," I assured her. "A steak sandwich and a beer sounds great."

The Colonial Grill was almost filled to capacity. At least I knew lunch would be good. The aroma of barbeque wafted throughout. We claimed a chunky wooden table for two against the far wall.

A waitress was on us almost immediately. Carol declined the menu and ordered her steak sandwich medium with mushroom. I asked for mine medium-rare with peppers and cheddar. A Corona for me, a sour apple martini for her.

As soon as the waitress was gone, Carol said, "I'm really glad you came. I had actually been considering calling you since we got the news about Brian this morning. But I'm not sure I would have, so it's good that you stopped by."

"I figured it was probably him, but I wasn't positive," I said. "He was so young. What could he have done to deserve that?"

"Brian was a pretty conservative young man. I doubt that he did anything. I'm figuring it was more like he knew something." She looked across at me and waited to see if I agreed.

I nodded. "Do you have any ideas?"

She sighed heavily. "I'm afraid the reason I wanted to see you was that I was hoping *you* could shed some light on it all for *me*." She snorted and shook her head. "I'm so naïve," she said. "You know, I actually thought all that police stuff was silly. I really believed that Connor just dove too deeply and cracked his skull. And as a matter of fact, I'm still not convinced that that's not exactly what did happen. But Brian…" She shook her head again.

The waitress returned with our drinks. Carol wasted no time taking a long pull on hers. Then she continued.

"You know, it isn't that I'm not saddened to hear about Brian," she said, "but I think what's really got me upset today is… if he was… well, obviously he wasn't an accident. So if *he* wasn't an accident, then that puts Connor's… thing… in a whole new light."

Suddenly Carol's eyes welled. She wiped them with a napkin, apparently unconcerned about the small amount of makeup she had applied earlier in the day. Then she took another long drink of her martini, draining the glass to about half way down.

"I have the dog," I heard myself say, and it sounded every bit as misplaced as it was.

"Yeah, I know," she said, seemingly unconcerned about that. "Now that Brian's… If you're interested in keeping the dog, you should call Ellen. I'm sure you could work something out."

She looked across at me again. It wasn't the dog that was on her mind.

I wanted to lighten her up a bit. "So when did Kevin figure out that I was the investigator?"

She wiped her eyes again but started laughing at the same time. "He's such a jerk," she said. When she looked back at me again she laughed harder still, and I had to resist the urge to laugh myself.

Our sandwiches arrived. As I was lifting mine to my mouth, I noticed that Carol was still looking at hers.

"Hey, this was your idea," I prompted. "Come on. You'll feel better."

She managed a smile and picked up the sandwich.

"So tell me about Connor," I said. "Anything at all. You never know what might prove useful."

"He was the nicest man I ever met," she said. "He was what I thought Kevin was going to be. But I know now that Kevin will never be like that. Connor was so… so *good.* He would do anything for anybody."

She stopped to take another couple of swallows of her drink. I chewed, looked back, and waited.

"It was just getting to be golf weather too," she continued. "When the weather was nice, we'd often play golf on Wednesdays. I'd get one of the college kids to work the store until mid-afternoon, and of course the doctor's office was closed on Wednesday, so we'd stop for breakfast and then play nine holes. Ellen doesn't play, and Kevin would rather go sailing, which I think is okay, but I much prefer golf."

"I can understand why you feel so badly about losing him."

"My own father died when I was eleven," she confided. "I don't mean to get too psychoanalytical, but maybe in a way, Connor was… you know."

"That's interesting," I said. "I understand that Brian's father abandoned him while he was just a kid and then his mother died too. Did Brian and you ever share your feelings about what it was like to lose a parent at such an early age?"

"Not really," she said. "Brian was never very close to anyone in the family except Connor. In fact, I guess there was a history with Kevin and Tim. I don't know; I've never fully understood it myself. But anyway, no, Brian and I never had occasion to talk all that much."

She finished off her drink. I waited, hoping she'd pick up where she left off. She did.

"But I did go to see his band a couple of times." she said more cheerfully.

I nodded my understanding before moving on. "What do you think of Dr. Golden?"

"Connor's best friend," she said. "They go back a long way."

I noticed she said "go," as though Connor Bradley were still alive. Not all that uncommon in the early going when someone has lost a loved one.

"I didn't know him that well," she continued. "Of course he was always at family functions, but you know how that works. The guys tend to gather together and the women... Or else it's by age, you know? He always seemed pleasant enough, though."

"I'm going to feel a bit uncomfortable going here, but I think it's necessary," I prefaced. "Since Dr. Golden's wife died, have you noticed him paying more attention to Ellen?"

Carol snorted and her eyes went wide. "I didn't have to wait for his wife to die to notice *that*," she said. "I think everyone knew, probably including his wife." She thought for a moment. "I doubt that anything ever actually happened, though. His friendship with Connor was much too strong." She emitted a chuckle. "Besides, I can't picture Ellen having sex with *any*one. I've often wondered where her two kids came from."

The waitress came by and I asked for another martini and another Corona. Carol didn't object.

I finished off my sandwich and noticed that Carol had eaten only half of hers. It seemed that she wasn't going to bother with the other half.

"I hope I'm not responsible for your loss of appetite," I said.

She was staring down at the table and appeared not to have heard my comment. The waitress returned with our drinks and Carol went for hers immediately.

After placing it back down on the table, she slowly swirled the stem of the glass back and forth. "How can somebody take another life?" she wondered aloud. "It's... it's so final. And so wrong."

I simply nodded my agreement. Carol snorted and shook her head before speaking again.

"Did you know that when Ivan the Terrible was in power, he and his soldiers would attack a village and rape and murder and plunder, and then they'd go back to a church and pray for the souls of the people they'd killed?" She drained off a good portion of her drink and then declared, "People suck."

I smiled my amusement, which apparently caused her to laugh at herself.

"So what about you?" she asked more cheerfully. "I think I've told you about all I know and I've still got half a drink left. And I'm assuming that most of what you told me last week was less than the truth, you snake in the grass."

The next ten minutes consisted essentially of me coming clean about myself, and Carol finishing off her second martini. The only additional piece of information I gathered from her was that Library Science had been her minor. She reiterated that she really was from Minnesota and that she had attended Wellesley College.

While walking back to the bookstore, she at one point thought out loud that she'd have to ask "Cheryl" if she would come in at noon tomorrow. "Beauty day," she explained, adding with disgust, "Look at this hair." The hair looked fine to me, but what do we guys know?

I walked her all the way to the bookstore, and after she removed the sign with the cardboard clock, she turned to me and said, "Airedale. You're definitely an Airedale guy."

"I just might do that," I said. "Based upon your recommendation, of course."

"Feel free to drop by again next time you want to do lunch… or dinner… or whatever," she said.

I told her I just might do that too.

Carol Bradley had given me a lot to think about while walking back to my car. For one thing, like most other people, I knew that Ivan the Terrible was a sixteenth century Russian czar, but I didn't know that he used to pray for the people he had killed. Of course we all pick up rather useless bits of trivia here and there, but was it merely a coincidence that somebody else had mentioned Ivan the Terrible recently? Somebody in the same family, in fact. Ellen Bradley had told me that Brian did a paper on Ivan's reign. And yet Carol had just said that she and Brian never had much occasion to speak. Of course it could have gone from Brian to Connor and then from Connor to Carol. Or for that matter, Carol could have picked it up on the History Channel.

Then there was that comment about she and her father-in-law often going to breakfast before playing golf. I remembered that Brian had told me his uncle never ate breakfast outside his own house. Was that a *never* never? There would certainly be no way to ask him for a clarification now.

New questions aside, I again felt sorry for Carol Bradley. She was an even lonelier woman than I had previously realized.

I arrived back at my car still engrossed in thought and didn't bother to turn the ignition. Instead I continued to play back the conversation I'd just had with Carol. There was something else she had said, but I couldn't put a finger on it. But there was something; I was sure of it.

After spending another ten minutes failing to recall whatever it was, I started the car and pulled out of the parking space.

That was it! The parking space. I had been trying to recall everything she'd said over lunch, but it was way back when we were leaving the bookstore that it had happened. She seemed more concerned than might be expected about not wanting to leave her parking space.

I decided to change my plans. Dr. Golden and Ellen would be there tomorrow.

I backed the car back into the parking space, grabbed the Red Sox cap and sunglasses, fed the meter to cover the maximum two hours, and hoofed it back to Washington

Street. It was unlikely that one of her employees had come to relieve her so soon.

I knew there was a smoke shop on the block opposite Carol Bradley's bookstore. It had been awhile since I'd smoked my last cigar. Positioned with a clear view out the window, at an angle from which I could see the bookstore up the street, I sat and smoked and talked politics and sports with the proprietor and one of the other customers. Eventually the other customer left and I struck up a conversation with an older gentleman who had come in five minutes earlier. He talked to me about his days in WW II until long after my cigar was history. In fact a couple of other guys and two young women had come and gone while he was still talking.

Finally, with the war veteran and his buddies hiding out in a barn in Italy after being shot down, Carol Bradley emerged from her bookstore. She started off in the direction away from the smoke shop. I gave the old timer a "Gotta go. Take care." He was still talking as I opened the door and went out onto the sidewalk.

I stayed on the opposite side of the street and kept my distance. Following someone on foot was a lot easier than doing it in a vehicle.

Before she reached the corner, Carol stopped, opened the door, and slid in behind the wheel of her car—a dark green Lincoln Continental.

Chapter 16

I read the license plate number, then turned and headed back in the direction of the smoke shop. I briefly considered talking to either the proprietor there or the college girl working in the bookstore. Ultimately, I decided that neither was worth the risk of Carol Bradley being informed that someone who fit my description was inquiring about her.

The moment I got to the car, I pulled up Peter on his cell.

"Last I knew Carol Bradley was driving a white Avalon," I said. "What did I miss?" I gave him the registration number and he said he'd call me back.

I was five minutes from home, taking the Arlington Street exit when my phone rang.

"The Avalon was reported stolen at 9:33 a.m. on April 17th, and it was found torched at 2:04 a.m. on April 18th. The lift took place in the driveway of the residence and the torch job was discovered on Condor Street in East Boston."

"I don't have a calendar here. What day of the week was the 17th?"

"Friday, a week ago."

I thanked Peter, disconnected, and turned off the memo recorder.

Friday, a week ago, was the Friday following the Thursday night on which Carol and I had gone out to dinner. That was when I'd seen her get into the white Avalon.

I parked the car a few doors up from my building, and just before getting out, I heard the news about Brian. The body had been identified. Even though Carol had told me about it, hearing it on the radio was still disturbing.

I entered my building, anxious to sit myself in front of the computer and get it all down.

Cedric was waiting to greet me as enthusiastically as always. I'd been so caught up in the Bradley thing that I'd forgotten he'd have to eat and go out. After feeding him, I took him for a short walk to the corner of Clarendon Street and back.

When we returned, I downloaded the phone message I hadn't bothered with fifteen minutes ago. "Hello, Dean. This is Ellen Bradley. I have some news that I believe may be of interest to you. Please call and let me know if you will be able to meet with me tomorrow morning." She left her number.

I played the message again. And then I played it a third time. There was something in her voice that I could best describe as simply nervousness. Not quite fear, just a serious concern.

I wondered if her "news" was merely that Brian's body had been found. But surely she must have realized that I had to have seen or heard that on TV or radio.

I placed the call.

"Bradley residence."

"Mrs. Bradley, Dean Cello."

"Oh, Dean, I'm so glad that you called. The more I thought about it, the more I became convinced that you would indeed want to know about this. Is it at all possible that you could join me for tea at nine tomorrow morning?"

"Certainly, Mrs. Bradley. I'll definitely be there. But I must say you've peaked my curiosity. Is there any chance that you could give me a hint as to what this is about?"

"Not on the phone, Dean. I shall look forward to seeing you in the morning."

"Nine o'clock, then. I'll be prompt."

I hung up feeling that the way things were going I wouldn't be surprised to walk in and find Ellen Bradley's body on the floor of her kitchen at 9:00 a.m. tomorrow morning. Wouldn't Schmidlin love that.

I'd just opened The Doctor's Dog file when the phone rang.

"Sure, when I'm not there, you come home," Nicole said.

"Hey, I was home last night. The Common, your book about New Bedford, remember? Speaking of which, how's it going down there?"

"I love this job," she said. "But it occurs to me that I go to all these places without you. When you finish this current case you're working on, we should get away somewhere for a few days."

I told her I thought that sounded like a good idea.

She asked me if I'd caught the latest news about Brian and I told her I had. I also told her that I visited Dr. Meier and had lunch with Carol Bradley, without going into detail about either. Then I told her about Ellen's cliffhanger.

At the end of our conversation I said, "Well, at least I know there aren't any lumberjacks in New Bedford."

"No, but I met this Portuguese cook," she said.

We did our I-love-yous and she told me she'd call back again tomorrow. I had to promise that I wouldn't get myself killed in the meantime.

There was a lot of typing to do. I took all the new information I'd acquired and inserted each piece chronologically as best I could. As new thoughts came to me, I backed up and inserted them where they seemed to make the most sense. Then I did a separate synopsis on each of the individuals involved—Connor, Brian, each suspect; I even did one on Lieutenant Schmidlin.

When I turned off the computer, I noticed that it was dark outside. Cedric was asleep on the floor. I turned on the ballgame and half watched as the Sox beat Detroit 7 to 5. One more quick trip outside for my favorite beast, and then

I turned in, thoughts of the Bradley clan intermingling in my head.

On Friday morning, I ran, showered, and had just finished getting dressed when the phone rang.

"Same routine, same time, every day," said Nicole. "You'd be easy to assassinate." Then realizing what she had said, she started to laugh. "Oow, I kind of forgot about your current situation," she claimed.

"That Portuguese cook must have really been something."

Nicole got down to what she called about. "Hey, I, actually *we*, got an offer last night, and I don't want you to feel obligated, if you can't, you can't."

"What can't I do?"

"Dan and his wife have invited us to spend the weekend at their summer place in Harwich Port. I just thought, if it's possible I mean, that you might enjoy a break. But if you can't..."

Her careful approach made me realize how much I'd been neglecting her.

"I'll be there. Exactly where and what time?"

After I got the details, I hung up wondering—Why is it so easy to jumble up your priorities? But then, sure enough, even though I felt certain that I'd made the right decision, I immediately found myself again thinking about the Bradleys.

The Cape Cod plan called for me to meet Nicole and the Hardings for dinner at the Pequod at six. Cedric was invited too, but of course he'd have to wait in the car while we ate. Since Harwich Port was about halfway out on the hook, I'd have to leave Boston by four, and that was assuming there would be no serious traffic at the Sagamore Bridge. I had plenty of time for tea with Ellen Bradley, but little else.

I had told Ellen I would arrive promptly, so I took the liberty of ringing the bell five minutes early.

Pink man-tailored shirt and white cotton skirt—she was the picture of neatness, her aging-but-shapely feminine form displayed just enough to entice the imagination. It occurred to me that if a man could get past her eccentricity, which Dr. Golden had apparently done, it would easy to lust for her.

"Oh, Dean, I'm so glad that you could come."

And I'm so glad that you're still breathing. "Wouldn't miss it for the world. Top secret information *and* tea with a charming lady."

I do believe she blushed.

Apparently we had become familiar enough to have tea like normal folks. I was ushered into the kitchen, where the table was neatly set and the pot was already whistling.

"I'm very sorry to hear about Brian," I said.

Ellen motioned for me to sit down, then turned off the gas and grabbed a potholder.

"Well that's what I want to tell you about," she said while pouring.

"That Brian was found, you mean?"

"No, no," she assured me. "I'm sure you learned from the television that Brian is quite dead. But it's something about *how* he was killed. The poor boy."

There was that matter-of-fact "dead" thing again.

As she sat down adjacent to me, she motioned for me to help myself to the bagels and Danish that were on separate plates in the middle of the table. In fact, I hadn't eaten at home, precisely because I presumed she would want to feed me. I selected a lemon Danish.

"Well I heard the television version," I said, leaving the question implied.

Ellen made me wait while she sipped her tea. After she had returned the cup to its saucer, she leaned in conspiratorially.

"I received a call from that Lieutenant Schmidlin," she said. "Yesterday afternoon."

"Really," was the best I could do.

As she raised her cup to take another sip, I noticed that her hand had started to tremble some.

"Are you feeling alright, Mrs. Bradley?"

"I'm afraid I am a bit out of sorts," she admitted. "But this news… it's so awful."

"Take your time," I urged patiently.

"You're such a gentleman," she said. "Anyway, he wanted to come over here again. I told him I was meeting somebody for an early dinner, but he insisted that he had new information. Information that I would want to be made aware of, he said. Well naturally I asked him why he couldn't just tell me over the phone, and that's when he told me that it wasn't just about Brian. It was about Connor."

I had taken only one bite of my Danish, and I now placed it back down on the plate.

"So I postponed my dinner date and invited him to come over. Well not even a half-hour had passed when he appears at my door with a police officer in a uniform. A big tall man. I wanted to tell him that I didn't recall having invited anyone else, but then I figured 'Oh what the hell, Ellen.'"

Now her lip and chin were quivering. I took the liberty of reaching over and gently but firmly holding her hand. "Slowly take a deep breath," I urged her.

She did that, and then she continued. "Lieutenant Schmidlin told me that the police lab reported that a brick was found not far from where Brian had been murdered. He said that most of the blood on the brick was Brian's, but… but there was also blood on the brick that was from Connor."

Ellen Bradley closed her eyes and took another slow deep breath.

"Why do you think Lieutenant Schmidlin wanted you to know that?" I asked.

"Well at first I thought he just wanted me to think that he was hard at work on my husband's case," she said with an edge. "But before he left, he asked if he could use my phone. He called Dr. Howard Golden, Connor's best friend, and made arrangements to visit Howard too, which in fact he did immediately after leaving here."

"Did Dr. Golden later tell you what they talked about?"

"Well of course he did. And it was the same thing that was talked about here. Mr. Schmidlin told Howard about... the blood and then he asked him if he had any ideas?"

"Which of course he didn't."

"No. He's a doctor, not a policeman."

I patted her hand and urged her to drink her tea.

We spent the next twenty minutes eating and drinking while Mrs. Bradley graciously answered a few questions, which I posed as casually as I could. Under the guise of sympathy for Brian, I inquired about his relationships with several individual family members. Ellen said that he and Carol hardly ever spoke. It wasn't that there was any animosity; it was just that they appeared to have little in common. She remembered that Carol once went to see his band play, though. She said she remembered that happening because it had seemed so unusual.

I sandwiched in something innocuous and then, leading with Connor, asked about his relationships with his daughters-in-law. Ellen explained that while he got along well with both, she thought he had more in common with Carol. She also thought that Connor paid special attention to Carol in deference to the fact that she had lost her own father at an early age.

Ellen excused herself when the phone rang. Of course I was privy to only one side of the ensuing conversation.

"Extra Strength Tylenol, but I'm going to be leaving in a while."

Silence while the other party spoke.

"Oh, I'm afraid I'll be gone by then, Tim. Don't worry. I'll get it up in Maine. Why are you leaving at three today?"

Whatever Tim's answer, it caused Ellen to look confused, but then she shook her head dismissively. Evidently whatever he said wasn't worth challenging. She said goodbye.

Ellen hung up the phone and apologized to me again.

"I'm going up to York Beach for the weekend," she explained.

"Well don't let me detain you," I said placing my cup down.

"Oh, not at all," she insisted. "I'm not leaving until noon."

"Well just the same. I'm sure you have to get ready," I said, coming to my feet. "Thank you very much for the information, the tea, and especially for your company, Mrs. Bradley."

She smiled at me approvingly. "You and Nicole are such a delightful young couple," she said.

I was crossing the threshold, leaving the kitchen, when she called from behind. "Oh, I almost forgot," she said excitedly. "Cedric. Nicole told me how fond of him you are. Now that Brian is…" She paused and smiled warmly. "I want you to keep him."

Somehow I hadn't thought about Cedric while I was there. I was speechless.

"And here, you might as well take this," she added. She handed me a can of dog food that she had just picked up from the counter. "It appears to be the only one left. It was on the kitchen table the night…" She didn't want to finish the sentence. But now I had to know for sure.

"Two Saturdays ago?"

She nodded affirmatively.

"Mrs. Bradley, did you by any chance mention the can of dog food on the kitchen table to Lieutenant Schmidlin?

"No," she answered innocently. "I don't even know when I noticed it."

I went back to Cedric.

"Mrs. Bradley, you've got to allow me to pay you something for a champion Airedale."

"Nonsense," she insisted. "You've worked hard enough already. You deserve him no matter what."

I thanked her profusely and bid her an enjoyable weekend up at York.

Back in the car, my mind was on overload again. I drove around the corner and down about half a mile to the parking lot of the White Hen Pantry where I'd bought the town paper a week ago. I had to think.

Brian's call had been left on my machine at 6:23 and he had said that he'd already explained to his uncle that he had Cedric. And since Connor got out a can of dog food, Brian must have said that he was bringing Cedric over, probably on the way to his gig. In fact Ellen had earlier confirmed that the dog was there when she left for the mall. But apparently he never got to eat. And then, for some reason, I two days later find Cedric in Brian's condo.

If nothing else, the dog food thing, as well as the brick, seemed to confirm the logical conclusion that both victims were killed within a very short span of time. Perhaps even at the *same* time!

My thoughts shifted to Ellen and Dr. Golden being questioned by Schmidlin with a uniformed officer present.

It seemed unlikely that Ellen was going up to York Beach alone. Dr. Golden? The most direct route from his house to Ellen's would take him right by the variety store where I was parked. And then they would drive by again in the opposite direction to take Route 1 north to Interstate 95.

I still had a couple of hours before getting packed to go to the Cape.

I backed the car into a space off to the side. It could be awhile, but I had to know. Fortunately the sports talk show on the radio was relatively entertaining.

At 11:47 the black Mercedes went by with Dr. Howard Golden at the wheel. At 12:06 it went back out again with Ellen Bradley in the shotgun seat. I was ecstatic that she'd given me the dog, but her husband, who by all accounts was a terrific guy, had been dead for only twelve days, and there they were again. For the weekend this time.

I should have headed home then, but the adrenalin was pumping. I found myself driving toward Wakefield Center. Although Dr. Meier had all but eliminated Tim as a serious suspect, he was leaving at three today, and whatever his explanation was, his mother didn't seem to think it was credible. I couldn't stop; I was on a roll.

The silver-blue Saab was in its usual spot. I drove down a way and backed into one of the angle parking spaces on the opposite side of the street, and then I went into a lunch spot for a BLT. I was working hard; screw my arteries.

The walk along the lake took another hour or so. It was 2:40 when I got back to the car and started keeping an eye on the pharmacy. At 3:01 Tim Bradley emerged and got into his car.

Given a choice, I'd have preferred not to be in the Volvo, but at the same time I was beginning to feel invincible. Besides, the worst thing that could happen was he'd notice me, which meant I'd start my trip to the Cape on schedule.

But if Tim Bradley had been watching for a tail recently, he didn't show any sign of it. Out to Route 1, south onto the Northeast Expressway. How lucky could I get? He was heading toward Boston. On the highway it was easy to change lanes and keep an eye on him without getting too close. We crossed the Mystic River on the Tobin Bridge, but then, instead of heading into Boston proper, Bradley exited toward Charlestown. If he were going to notice me it would be on the exit ramp. I let a Buick get in between. At the corner, his Saab was the first car at the light. I reached over and popped the glove compartment for the Red Sox cap and sunglasses. The light turned green and the Saab turned left. The Buick went straight through the intersection. I took the left and was right behind him now. I tried to keep a distance as we proceeded down Constitution Road, past Old Ironsides, and into the heart of what used to be the Charlestown Naval Shipyard. The old brick buildings had been refurbished as condos now. Evidently one of them was our destination.

When he pulled into a parking space, I did the same about a half block back and on the opposite side of the street. Tim Bradley got out of his car, walked up to one of the buildings, and then disappeared into the narrow brick portico.

After waiting a couple of minutes, I drove three-quarters of the way around the block and parked on the adjacent street, facing back out toward Constitution Road. I got out and walked down to the building I'd seen Bradley enter.

Built into the brick wall on the right side of the portico was a cluster of twelve numbered mailboxes with a doorbell positioned under each one. I started at Number 12 and worked my way backward. When the respective owners asked who was ringing, I told each, "I need to speak to Tim Bradley." I got responses such as "You've got the wrong unit," and "There's nobody here by that name," and "Never heard of him." But on Number 7, I got a different kind of response—"Who's looking for him?"

Jason Toohig. I descended the four brick steps and walked away quickly, turning the nearby corner. After circling three quarters of the same block I'd just driven around, I climbed into the Volvo and headed back out Constitution Road. Nobody was behind me.

It took only ten minutes to get home from Charlestown.

I gave Cedric a cursory greeting and rushed to the phone to call Peter.

"Hey, I'm glad you called," he said. "I was thinking. Do you want me to get Frank to ram Kevin Bradley's wife's new car?"

"Thanks, but I'd rather you do me a different favor. See what you've got on a Jason Toohig." I spelled the name and gave him the address.

"Sounds urgent," he said with no indication of sarcasm. When business became serious, he turned humorless in a heartbeat. He said he'd call me right back. I told him to give me ten minutes; I had to feed Cedric and get him out.

When I hung up the phone, Cedric was standing by looking up at me, tail vibrating. He was my dog now. I decided to wait until later to tell him.

My watch said ten minutes before four. No way I'd be out on schedule. I emptied a can of dog food into Cedric's bowl and hastily started packing while he ate.

Fifteen minutes later we were back from our walk. No message yet.

I resumed packing my suitcase and was just zipping it up when the phone rang.

"Congratulations, pal," said Peter. "Looks like you left clicked in the right place."

Chapter 17

Peter's reading of Jason Toohig's sheet was at the same time both encouraging and alarming.

"Sale of alcohol to a minor, possession of marijuana, possession of cocaine, possession of cocaine with intent to distribute, two counts of assault and battery, and assault with a dangerous weapon. All in the Chicago area. He did some time out there. By the way, sorry it took me a few extra minutes to get back. I called a Sergeant Stephen Bauer out there. Bauer says he knows Toohig firebombed his ex-girlfriend's house too, but the DA said he didn't have enough to prosecute." Peter took a breath before asking, "Did you see the news this morning?"

"Yeah, Nicole called," I said. "And I got the ID later on the radio."

"Toohig's assault with a dangerous weapon… You want to guess what the weapon was?"

Somehow it actually took me a minute to make the connection. "A brick."

"A brick."

I sighed audibly. "I spent seventy-five bucks on a bottle of wine and had your Dr. Meier all but exonerate Tim Bradley this morning. And now this afternoon I follow Bradley to Toohig's condo in Charlestown."

"Meier," scoffed Peter. "What does he know? He thinks I'm crazy."

I wasn't in a laughing mood. I heard myself sigh a second time. "I'm committed to going to the Cape for the weekend," I said in frustration.

"Actually that doesn't make me sad," Peter said quite seriously. "This Toohig isn't a deadbeat dad, Dean. This guy's bad. You need to be careful."

"No schoolteacher jokes?"

"Not this time."

I thanked Peter, disconnected, and looked at my watch. It was twelve past four. No need to call yet. I might still be able to make it.

Cedric spent the first ten miles or so with his head out the window, ears blowing back in the breeze. Every once in a while I took my mind off the Bradley case long enough to rejoice in the fact that he was my dog. I would take great care of him.

At the Sagamore Bridge the traffic slowed just enough to cause me to concede defeat and call Nicole. I'd be about a half-hour late.

As I pulled into the parking lot at the Pequod, I told myself to forget about the Bradleys and Jason Toohig and the Drs. Golden and Meier. I cracked the back windows a couple of inches and told Cedric to take a nap; I'd be back in awhile.

The maitre d' escorted me to the table at which Nicole and the Hardings were seated, and Nicole and Dan Harding both rose as Nicole did the introductions. Dan's wife's name was Maureen. I said it to myself three times. Not Carol, not Ellen, not Jill. Maureen.

"But we all call her 'Mo,'" said Dan.

"Nice to meet you, Mo."

The Hardings were fortyish and I knew they had two little girls who sometimes stayed with their grandmother for the weekend.

"You made pretty good time from the canal," said Nicole, who looked happy to see me.

I reached over to give her a kiss. "Well it's still off season," I said. "Besides, with you waiting, how could I not hurry?"

The waiter appeared and asked me if I'd care for a drink.

A quick glance around the table revealed that the others were already imbibing. I asked for an amaretto on the rocks.

"It was very nice of you folks to invite us down here for the weekend," I offered. "Especially with the dog."

Mo was the first to respond. "Well he's a champion. We're honored." Everybody laughed.

"He's okay in the car like that, huh?" asked Dan.

"Yeah, he just looks like any other dog," Nicole chimed in. "Dean only makes him wear his medal around in the house." Laughter again. I wondered how many they had had before I got there.

My amaretto arrived. I nodded to the waiter and took it in hand.

"Well actually, as of this very day, there has been a change in his status," I prefaced. With all eyes on me, I raised my drink and announced, "I had tea with Ellen Bradley this morning, and as of around ten o'clock or so, the name became Cedric Cello, thank you." A mixture of laughter and cheers went up. Nicole's eyes went wide as she beamed at me. I knew she was happy for me, but I also knew that she was as fond of Cedric as I was.

Fortunately, the Hardings were pretty down-to-earth people, not at all the pretentious suburbanites I feared they might be. We all enjoyed a leisurely lobster dinner, and the conversation was pleasant enough.

After dinner, we went out to my car and I introduced the Hardings to Cedric. Mo thought he was "so cute" and Dan said he was "a handsome dog." Despite their lavish praise, Cedric paid most of his attention to Nicole, whom he hadn't seen since yesterday morning.

Nicole and Cedric and I followed the Hardings to their beachfront "cottage," a Cape Cod style house that was tastefully furnished in American Country. Dan lighted the woodstove to take off the night air chill and we sat around drinking coffee and tea and chatting softly in the glow of the fire.

When it was time to retire for the evening, Dan said, "You two lovebirds can use the last bedroom down on the right. If you get up first in the morning, feel free to cook, make coffee, whatever. Make yourselves at home."

We thanked him and then we did indeed make ourselves at home in the guest bedroom.

Bright and early on Saturday morning Cedric and I ran the beach. Alone with my thoughts, I found myself going back over the same questions again. And again I came up with the same non-answers. But I decided the weekend on the Cape might actually do me some good. If I could put it all aside for a while, I might be able to come back to it with a clearer head later.

By the time Cedric and I got back, everyone was seated around the kitchen table having breakfast. Dan and Mo planned to hit the golf course; they welcomed us to either join them or feel free to go off on our own. Although Nicole was a fairly proficient golfer, I hadn't played since I'd wrapped a five iron around a maple tree a few years back. I liked to think I had grown since then, but just in case, I was delighted when she suggested tennis. We all agreed to meet for dinner at seven.

While driving to the tennis courts, I found myself wondering what Dr. Golden and Ellen Bradley were doing at that very moment up at York Beach.

"Mm, smell those blossoms," Nicole said. "Exactly what is that?"

"I can't say. I don't smell anything," I admitted.

"You really can't smell that?" she asked in amazement.

"No, but that's understandable. Women have a better sense of smell than men."

Nicole said she had not previously been aware of that tidbit, and I didn't expect her life to be changing dramatically now that she was.

Despite my efforts to the contrary, I found myself again

thinking about the Bradleys. Could the Tim Bradley-Jason Toohig connection be simply drugs? Toohig's record included the use of a brick, though. Odd weapon of choice.

"I love those high white Cape Cod fences with the rhododendrons growing along them," Nicole observed.

"Yeah, those are nice, aren't they?"

Why had Carol Bradley followed me the night of the Parents Club meeting? If in fact that was Carol's dark green Continental.

Ivan the Terrible?

"Oh, look at that big front porch," she implored passionately. "I love front porches. They're so warm and inviting."

I had to make an effort. "So exactly what's the difference between a porch and a deck?"

"A porch has a roof and a deck is open."

"Uh-huh. So what's a piazza?"

"I think it's an Italian porch."

"Okay. Then what's a verandah?"

"Drive the car, Dean."

I turned back and looked at Cedric. He looked like he was laughing too.

Tennis was good; it made me concentrate. In fact I actually won more than half the games. They don't let us do that anymore, right?

Later, we played on the beach with Cedric. In a few more weeks there would be droves of tourists and that wouldn't be possible.

On Saturday night, the four of us enjoyed a splendid dinner at the Ancient Mariner. I managed to keep my mind off the case until Mo divulged that Dan was obsessive about getting things ready in advance. Not only did he lay out his work clothes the night before, but he'd also been known to set the dinner table in mid-afternoon and once even put the paste on his toothbrush an hour before using it!

Although I too joined in on the frivolity, there was something in that revelation that bothered me. But somehow I couldn't yet pinpoint exactly what it was.

It wasn't until we got back to the house and I saw Cedric standing beside the kitchen table that the bell went off. Why would you take out a can of dog food if you weren't going to feed the dog right then and there? If you were like Dan, you could take it out in anticipation of the dog getting there, but in this case the dog was back and gone again and presumably still hadn't eaten. Unless of course Ellen had been less than truthful about the dog having been returned in the first place. But why?

On Sunday morning Nicole and I joined the Hardings in church. I found that I actually remembered when to kneel, stand, and sit. Most of the time.

Afterward Nicole and I browsed through the downtown section. I wandered into a bookstore and found a book about Airedales. Later in the day, I wowed everyone with all sorts of useless information: The name Airedale was taken from a valley in Yorkshire; the Airedale was the largest of the terriers and hence was known as the "King of the Terriers;" they were originally bred to catch rats, but were later used to hunt bears; and in World War I the British used them to run messages on the front lines. What guys!

When the merriment finally subsided, Nicole and I offered our heartfelt thanks and hit the highway.

"So what does Linda's wedding dress look like?" Nicole asked.

I shrugged. "I don't know."

Nicole shook her head but managed a smile. "And I suppose you don't know where the reception is going to be either."

"I'm sure it'll be on the invitation."

We rode in silence for a few minutes.

"Oh, look at *that* front porch," she said, turning to admire it longer as we passed.

"Oh, yeah, that's a beauty," I agreed without looking.

"Alright, Cello, let's have it."

"What?"

"I'm not saying you didn't do a good job of pretending, because you did. In fact there were times when you actually managed to *be* there this weekend."

"Do you think the Hardings could tell?"

"They don't know you like I do."

"How well do you know me?"

"Well enough to know that you've made some progress with your case and as a result you're even more obsessed than you were before. So go ahead; I'm listening."

"I don't deserve you."

"Obviously. But for some reason, I love you. Now let's hear it."

I filled Nicole in on all that she had missed, which I later realized was quite a bit.

As usual, she listened attentively before volunteering her opinion.

"Well obviously Schmidlin suspects Ellen and Golden."

"Right," I agreed. "He brought a uniformed officer with him while he leaned on each of them separately. He didn't yet have enough to obtain a warrant, but he was hoping."

We discussed an assortment of possibilities that all seemed to fall short, but the conversation was still useful in that it provided a good overview, and in the end it allowed me to finally put it all on a shelf for awhile.

For the rest of the way home we talked about the Hardings, Frank Capachietti, Peter's upcoming wedding, the likelihood of him having kids, the general upkeep that houses required, Cape Cod fences, and front porches. Nicole also mentioned that she was going up to Derry, New Hampshire to visit her parents next Sunday; I was welcome to come along if I wanted to.

We stopped in the North End for a Regina's pizza to take

home. The night had again turned cool. I lighted the marble corner fireplace and we ate the pizza in front of it on the floor of the study. Somewhere around one in the morning, we got up off the floor and went to bed.

Peter called as I was getting in from my run on Monday morning.

"Thought you'd want to know that I paid an off-the-record visit to your buddy Jason Toohig on Saturday morning. By the way, close acquaintances call him 'J.T.'"

"You inquired about his whereabouts on the night the doctor drowned, right?"

"Yep. Said he went to see the nephew's band that night. Met up with Tim Bradley there. So I checked that out. The bartender who was on says the band was booked there for the four weekends in April. He remembers two guys who fit their description because they came the week before and the week after too. They never came in together, just met at a table off to the right and in the rear."

"The band doesn't start until nine. Where was he earlier?"

"He claims he was home alone watching television. I asked him what he watched and what it was about. It checked out."

"What do you think?"

"If it weren't for that damn brick my hunch would be that he's clean on this one. If he's lying, he's much better at it than most. Of course home alone watching TV isn't an airtight alibi."

After we disconnected I closed my eyes and tried to put myself back in Brandy's a week ago Saturday night. I knew Tim Bradley had spent some time talking to a guy at a table in the back; I just couldn't remember what the guy looked like. But I did recall that their conversation took place during the last half-hour or so before Tim left. It was Tim Bradley's Saab that followed me that night, but the job on the Z4 was probably the handiwork of the infamous J.T.

I did my coffee and the sports page routine before adding the additional information to the case file.

Back in the recliner, I sipped at a second cup of coffee while considering my options. I decided to pay Carol Bradley another visit.

I called first to make sure she would be there. The girl who answered said she was due in at noon.

It was almost quarter past twelve when I found a space on Washington Street, just a few doors up from the bookstore. As I closed the car door, I turned and saw the dark green Continental passing by. It pulled into the next available parking space, three cars further up the block. I strolled over to the sidewalk and waited for Carol to emerge.

When she spotted me, she flashed that winning smile and outstretched her arms. "So nice to see you again," she gushed.

Her arms were still extended when she got to me. I accommodated her by loosely wrapping my arms around her while she gave me a hug. It was a friendlier hug than I might have anticipated—I felt one of her legs press up against mine.

When she released her grip she said, "I'm sorry; I can't go to lunch today." Then before I could speak, she added, "And tonight I promised a friend…" She dismissively waved her hand back and forth. "Anyway, today's not good. But I'm really happy to see you again."

We started to walk toward the bookstore.

"When did you get the Lincoln?" I asked.

"Oh, my old car got stolen and totaled," she casually explained. "I like this one better anyway. Can you stay and have a cup of coffee with me?"

"Sure," I agreed. "How do you take it? I'll run down to the center."

"Cream, one Sweet 'n Low," she said, still gushing as though I was some long lost lover. "Hurry back," she sang.

She had always been extra friendly, but this time she was outdoing herself. And incongruously enough, it was the first time she didn't have time for lunch or dinner.

I headed off to the center to get the coffees.

The bell made its now familiar sound as I entered the bookstore and Carol turned and smiled at me once again.

"One regular, one black. Let's do it," I said.

She gave me that mischievous look. "I've been waiting two weeks to hear you say that," she playfully proclaimed.

"But not tonight, huh?"

"Unfortunately, I'm going to be tied up for a couple of days. Why don't you give me a call toward the end of the week."

"Inventory?" I asked.

"No," she answered. "But I'll be working here late tonight and then I've got this friend who's going through something. I think she needs me right now."

"Can't get in the way of friendship."

"And tomorrow I have to go to the wake," she added.

I had checked the paper and noticed that the wake was indeed scheduled for Tuesday, not Monday.

We drank our coffees and engaged in superficial conversation for the next fifteen minutes—It was the time of year when business started to slow down; in the summer she sometimes worked shorter hours; she wished she lived in a warmer climate.

I stepped behind the counter far enough to toss my empty cup into the wastebasket and said, "I'll call you in a couple of days then."

She reached over and pulled my face toward her. She gave me a short but sensuous kiss, and then, still holding onto me, said, "I'll look forward to it." Again she smiled the smile of the seductress. My return smile might have been more one of amusement; I hoped it didn't show.

I walked to my car, got in, drove halfway around the block, parked again, and got out. I went into the neighborhood hardware store and bought an awl and a cigarette lighter. After walking back to Washington Street from the direction up from the bookstore, I pretended to have dropped something while passing behind Carol's car. As I ostensibly bent down to pick it up, I heated the tip of the awl and melted a small hole through one of her taillights. Standing up again, I examined the non-existent object I'd picked up, and pretended to put it in my pocket before continuing across the street. Then I returned to my car.

If Carol was really going to be working late, that meant she would be leaving in the dark. I just had to know.

Smelling blood now, I splurged and went back to the car rental place. The only SUV available was a Pathfinder in dark green. Fitting, I thought.

I drove back to Washington Street and pulled into a space down from the bookstore and Carol's parked car. If she really were going to leave work late, this would be a long one. I called Nicole at work and explained that I thought I might be onto something and could be late getting home.

At least I had the smoke shop. As long as I remained vigilant, I could always dash out from there and make it to the Pathfinder in time to follow.

After one cigar and several conversations with strangers, I took advantage of being the only customer in the place and approached the proprietor. I showed him my license and asked if he minded me using his establishment for an impromptu stake out. He said he didn't mind and recommended some Dominicans he had just gotten in. I bought the cigars.

Eventually, I grew tired of the smoke shop and returned

to the Pathfinder. At least one question had been answered; Carol was really working late.

It was early dusk when she finally emerged and headed up the street toward her car. She started the Continental, and from more than half a block back, I started the Pathfinder. Her lights went on, and as she pulled out of the parking space, I could see that the small but clearly visible point of white light was beaming out from the center of the otherwise red taillight. I didn't need it yet, but I might by the time we got where we were going.

She motored west out to 128, and now I could no longer make out the car, but I continued to follow that conspicuous white point of light. It turned south onto Route 1, and then headed over the expressway toward the city.

When it climbed up onto the Tobin Bridge I felt my heart start to pound.

It was no surprise when it exited into Charlestown. Up Constitution Road.

I didn't really have to go any further, but of course I did. I had to see it for myself. And then I did.

The dark green Continental sedan that had followed me last Monday night stopped at the residence of one Jason "J.T." Toohig.

Chapter 18

When I turned the corner from Arlington Street onto Beacon Street, I realized that I didn't remember a single thing about my drive home. I had been on some kind of automatic pilot, obsessed with thoughts and images of Carol Bradley, Jason Toohig, bloody bricks, and Connor Bradley and his unfortunate nephew Brian. A plausible hypothesis was that Carol had met Toohig through Tim, who probably had no idea that she had contracted him to kill her father-in-law and his nephew. But why? It couldn't be about money; the doctor's wife was presumably his beneficiary and she was still alive. And what about Brian? It had to be something they knew.

I hurriedly climbed the steps of my building, the adrenalin still pumping. I thought about how Carol had kissed me and brushed her leg up against mine earlier in the day. She had been playing me all along. In fact, when I first met her, I had just come from her sister-in-law's art gallery, where Jill had seen me up close and watched me drive away in the blue Z4. Could it be that I had gone into the bookstore as the hunter and come out as the prey?

As I slid my key into the lock, I briefly wondered if Nicole would pick up the scent of Carol's perfume. A silly thought; I dismissed it immediately. Besides, I would tell it like it was.

Nicole opened the door before I did and greeted me with a hug. She might not have picked up anything herself, but there was someone there who had an even keener sense of smell than a woman. Cedric spotted me from the study and came racing over in his usual style, tail wagging frantically. But when he reached where I stood, his tail dropped as he sniffed the leg of my pants. And then he did something I had never seen him do before. He growled.

After I changed my pants, the three of us sat in the study and I tried to remain as calm as possible while I related everything to Nicole. She listened patiently, but in the end had no ideas. The best advice she could give me was, "Be careful." After, she went into the computer and I turned the ballgame on, but I didn't have a clue who was pitching, how many outs there were, or even what the score was. Nevertheless, images of baseball players flickered in front of me while two male voices bantered about balls and strikes and whatever else while my mind raced in circles.

When Nicole got up from the computer, I moved in. Maybe adding the new information to the case file would trigger something in my head.

Eventually Nicole said she was going to bed; she had to go to work in the morning. I told her I was wide-awake and probably would be for most of the night. She kissed the top of my head and left me with my temporary insanity.

A glass of wine. Yes, that was it. The last time, when I solved the big one, I had been sipping at a glass of wine when I suddenly heard the full choir of angels sing the long "Ah" in three-part harmony.

I got up and poured myself a glass of Chianti. Same chair, same glass, same wine. The notes. I needed the notes. Printed. I got up and printed the entire case file from the doctor's call on the rainy Friday afternoon through what I'd just recorded a couple of hours ago.

I sat back down in the recliner with the glass of Chianti and the notes. I started reading and sipping. I read the entire file. Then I read it again. Then I started concocting possible scenarios. Most of them were wild, but I followed them through anyway. And in every case, they made no sense in the end.

I didn't remember falling asleep, but when I awoke at four-thirty, the rush was gone. The room was still. My heart rate was back to normal. In fact I inexplicably felt an all-embracing calm, an utterly total relaxation, as though I had slept for an eternity and awoken completely rejuvenated. And then, when I remembered why I had fallen asleep in the study, I understood. There it was. There had been no choir of angels this time, at least not that I could remember. It was simply there. As though I had known all along.

I felt a faint smile of satisfaction cross my lips as I sat there and began planning my attack.

By the time the early morning sun peeked through the window, I had it all mapped out. There would be just a few preliminaries I'd have to check out before actually going into battle.

When Cedric emerged from the bedroom and entered the study, I looked at the clock. It was seven straight up. He had come to get me.

We returned from our run to find Nicole in the kitchen. She had not gone upstairs to take her shower before breakfast the way she did over the prior seven months. Then I realized she hadn't done that all of last week either. I must have been so preoccupied that I hadn't noticed.

"Did you get any sleep?" she asked.

"Enough," I nodded.

She looked at me skeptically. "Are you okay?"

"No problem. The little man took care of everything."

It took her a moment. "Ah, the monopoly guy in the brain."

"The little man strikes again."

After I showered, Nicole had a bowl of Special K and I had toast and coffee while I presented my theory to her. When I saw her staring back and gently nodding, I knew it wasn't just my imagination.

"You're going to have to check out a couple of things before you go for it," she reminded me.

"I'll take care of that today," I told her. "Besides, the wake is this afternoon and tonight, so I'm on hold until tomorrow anyway."

Nicole got up from the table and opened the upper cabinet to the left of the stove. She pulled out some papers and started going through them until she found the one she was looking for. She held it up for me to see—my Aunt Lucy's biscotti recipe. She had remembered that back in September, on the morning when I confronted the killer, I had treated her for the first time to Aunt Lucy's biscotti.

"Are you going to pick up the anise extract or should I?" she asked.

Why not? Red Auerbach had his cigar; Dean Cello has Aunt Lucy's biscotti.

"I'll take care of it," I told her.

After Nicole showered and went off to work, I did my sports page thing. I'd missed a good ballgame. The Sox rallied in the eighth and held on to win by one in the ninth.

After folding up the paper and placing it down on the table lamp, I went to the phone and called Ellen Bradley.

"Excuse me, Mrs. Bradley, Dean Cello. I hope you enjoyed your weekend up at York Beach."

"Oh, we had an absolutely marvelous time, Dean, thank you. Of course it's still a bit cool up there in April, but we made the most of it despite the weather."

"Great. Glad to hear it. I apologize for bothering you, but I do have one new question, if I may."

"Don't be silly, Dean. You're never bothering me. What can I do for you?"

"Well I'm afraid it's a bit personal, so if you don't want to answer I certainly understand, but I must say it could very well be quite important."

"Oh? Well please do ask, Dean."

"Well it's about your husband Connor. I was wondering… Had he been acting differently lately? Say over the past few months or so?"

"Differently? How do you mean?"

"Well, admittedly, I'm not sure. Perhaps a bit detached.

But not *necessarily* that. Actually, anything at all that was seemingly out of character for him."

"How extraordinary," she proclaimed in hushed surprise. "Detached. Yes I think that's the perfect word for the way Connor had been for several months. But he had actually come back to normal during the past month or so."

"Thank you so much, Mrs. Bradley. Do have a pleasant day."

"But what does it mean?" she wanted to know. "How did you know that?"

"Right now I'm just working on a theory," I told her. "But if it pans out, I promise you'll be hearing." Before she could respond, I added, "Cedric gives his regards. Thanks again. Take care now," and disconnected.

I had one more call to make before leaving the house. The secretary answered and I went straight to work.

"Good morning. I'm Dean Cello. I saw Dr. Meier last Thursday. I wonder if you would be so kind as to ask him to give me a call."

She asked for my number; I gave it to her.

"He should have a free ten minutes just before eleven," she said.

I thanked her and told her I would wait.

At five minutes before eleven, the phone rang.

"Mr. Cello, Dr. Benjamin Meier. What can I do for you?"

"Thank you for returning my call, Doctor. I have just one question if I may."

"I have an opening at two," he said. "Why don't you come by then?"

"As I say, it's just one question…"

"No problem. I'll see you then."

Rather mercenary, I thought, but he was the man with the answer I needed.

At two o'clock, I brought Dr. Meier a relatively inexpensive bottle of Merlot. It was only one question after all. This time the doctor gave me the answer I was looking for. I thanked him and left further encouraged.

Although I could have picked up a bottle of anise extract locally, I drove to Lynnfield for it. There was something I had to find out at the White Hen Pantry on Main Street.

The trip to Lynnfield having been successfully completed, the only thing left to do now was to run it all by Peter.

Peter and I met at a place on Market Street in Brighton, where he sipped his coffee and listened without interrupting for a solid ten minutes. When I was finished, he continued to look at me for a moment. Then he smiled wryly and nodded his approval. He asked the question totally devoid of any sarcasm.

"This came a long way from a lost dog, didn't it?"

"It's a keeper," I agreed. "I just hope I can pull it off."

We took another five minutes to fine-tune the particulars.

As much as I would have liked to pay my respects, going to Brain's wake was out of the question. Instead, Nicole and I took Cedric for a walk along the esplanade, after which she ran an errand on Newbury Street while I went home and watched the ballgame. This time I knew what was going on.

Wednesday morning started out like any other morning. Cedric and I took our run, which we extended at the back end without effort. It was now the last week in April; the magnolias were in bloom along Commonwealth Avenue, and the sun was rising earlier and warming the air up sooner.

When I came out of the shower, Nicole had just removed the last log of biscotti from the oven and was beginning to slice it.

"You even did the baking?"

"Oh, I wasn't even thinking that you did it last time. Is it okay?"

"It's more than okay," I assured her. "Thanks."

We ate more biscotti than we probably should have. As usual, I dunked a couple of mine in the black coffee. Nectar of the gods.

I bounced the plan off Nicole one more time to try to tie up any loose ends I might have missed.

Before Nicole went off to work, she cautioned, "Since I'll be working late tonight, I won't see you again until it's over. Be careful. Don't take any unnecessary chances. Be very careful."

After I had my coffee and read the paper, I called the bookstore.

"She's supposed to be coming in at noon," the girl said.

At quarter past twelve, I called again. Carol answered.

"Carol, this is Dean Cello," I announced solemnly. "It's very important that I see you. What time are you closing the store tonight?"

"Hey, Dean," she said cheerfully. "Why wait till tonight? Why don't you stop by?"

I remained solemn. "I think I've figured it all out, Carol. I think I know who murdered your father-in-law and Brian both. I want to run my theory by you, but not in public. And not in the store during business hours. I'm afraid you might find what I have to tell you rather upsetting. Can I just come by at closing time?"

After hesitating some, she offered a tentative, "Sure." She sounded more confused than nervous. "I'll be locking up at six," she said.

"Great. I'll see you then. And Carol… You'd better not mention this to anyone until after we talk."

Carol agreed to keep our meeting secret, but I doubted that she would. In fact she would probably make arrangements to have J.T. hiding somewhere in the store just prior to my arrival. Just in case she needed him.

I considered what it might be like to be Carol Bradley

at that moment. If this Cello guy were really onto her, why wouldn't he just call the police? She didn't actually know him all that well. Maybe *she* should call the police. Too risky. She didn't know what he knew and she couldn't take a chance. Neither could she take a chance of not meeting with him, though.

I called Nicole and Peter to tell them it was a go for six o'clock. Nicole spared me another admonition to be careful and simply wished me good luck. Peter's manner was devoid of any foolishness; these were the moments he lived for.

I ate a couple more biscotti before walking over to the Copley library to check out the latest in my favorite science journals. Then I stopped at Angel's for a burger with French fries and a cola. If I died tonight, my restricted arteries wouldn't matter. After lunch I spent the rest of the afternoon in the Common with Cedric. While sitting on a park bench, I told him my plan. He'd be coming with me tonight. He deserved to be there.

At five o'clock, Cedric and I entered the smoke shop. If Jim, the proprietor, objected to the dog, I'd have to put him back in the car for an hour, but as it turned out that wasn't an issue; the two got along famously. I wanted to be across the street early because there was a chance Carol might panic and make a run for it. So far though, the store was still open. Customers were coming and going.

Around five-twenty, the World War II vet entered the smoke shop and picked up where he'd left off five days ago. He and the rest of the crew of his downed B-17 were walking along a dirt road in rural Italy when they spotted, casually walking toward them, a group of unarmed German soldiers. The Germans dashed into the woods on the left side while the Americans dashed into the woods on the right. The story provided an amusing anecdote, actually taking my mind off Carol Bradley and J.T. for a few minutes.

At five minutes before six, I bid my cigar-smoking friends

a good night and Cedric and I crossed the street to the bookstore.

We descended the six brick steps and I opened the door. It would be the last time I'd hear the bell chime.

Chapter 19

Carol smiled agreeably as she reached under the counter and then passed across the CLOSED sign. I hung it a couple of minutes early and locked the door. Carol glanced down at Cedric who had tucked his tail between his legs and was emitting a low steady growl. That was pretty much the reaction I'd expected.

"For some reason, that dog has never liked me," Carol stoically declared.

I ignored her inane comment. "Are you sure all the customers are out?"

"Absolutely," she said agreeably.

"Good. Then if you'll just come out from behind the counter…"

Her eyes narrowed, but she managed to hold a tentative smile. "You're acting strange," she said only half playfully.

I did my best to smile affably. "How about a hug?"

That suggestion elicited a more spontaneous response. She gave me that mischievous grin and we embraced. Then, while looking in her eyes at close range, I allowed my hands to run down the side of her rib cage and onto her hips. If she had a weapon, I didn't know where she could be hiding it.

"Is that what this is all about?" she murmured sensuously. "You want to seduce me in my place of business?"

"Not at all," I assured her, stepping back. "Like I said on the phone, I've figured out who murdered Connor, and then a short while later on the same night, Brian. I wanted you to be the first to know. Is there someplace we could sit down?"

"Of course," she said, now more serious.

I kept a close eye on her as she stepped back behind the

counter and passed me a wooden chair, then brought out another for herself.

As we took our seats, she said, apparently in jest, "I guess I should feel honored." But as she said it, I noticed her lower lip begin to quiver ever so slightly.

Cedric must have sensed something too; his growl grew louder.

"Cedric, quiet," I commanded. "Sit." He did as he was told, but he kept both eyes fixed on Carol.

"Do you know a man named Jason Toohig?" I asked her. "Actually, you probably refer to him as J.T."

Carol went pale. I let her labor in silence for a pregnant moment before helping her out.

"An acquaintance of your brother-in-law. Lives in one of the condo units at the old navy yard in Charlestown."

Carol gave a quick nod, as though her memory had been jogged. "Oh, yeah," she said. "It took me a minute. I don't know him that well. Tim introduced me once and… I guess I just forgot about him."

I nodded agreeably. "He won't be showing up here, by the way. He's been detained courtesy of the Boston Police Department. In fact, I would expect that by now he's pretty much told them everything in an effort to save himself. As you probably know, he's done time already. I'm sure he doesn't want to waste anymore of his life than he has to."

Carol's right hand had begun to shake. I saw a momentary flash of rage in her eyes. When she spoke again, her throat had gone dry and her voice trembled.

"I don't understand," she maintained. "Explain."

"Okay," I agreed. "Shortly after you were introduced to J.T., he boasted to you about what a bad guy he was. Guys like him boast about their crimes the way stockbrokers boast about getting in on the ground floor of a winner. They're proud of their accomplishments. It's how they define themselves. Anyway, to you this was a stroke of good fortune;

the timing couldn't have been better. You had someone you wanted dead, and now you had someone to do the job. So you hired Toohig to kill your father-in-law. But it had to look like an accident. Lessen the likelihood of an extensive investigation. So the illustrious J.T. tried. Twice in fact. But both times he screwed up. Maybe accidents weren't his specialty. Anyway, each time he failed, you became more incensed, more inpatient. So finally, you decided if you want a job done right you've got to do it yourself.

"On the Saturday night of the murder, you knew Ellen was going to be at the mall. You'd have a window of at least an hour. And you had a perfect alibi—a quid pro quo with your sister-in-law Jill, who was having an affair with a man in Gloucester. How could she say she wasn't at the movies with you without exposing herself? Of course she had no idea to what extent she was covering for you. And as long as she didn't know, she'd maintain that the two of you had gone to the movies together.

"You also knew that Connor took his swim every night about an hour after dinner. You had a perfect set-up. Ellen at the mall, Connor alone in the pool, and you ostensibly at the movies. But of course in reality you weren't at the movies. You were in Connor's house with a sidewalk brick in your handbag. You approached him while he was swimming. Upon seeing you, he of course began climbing out of the pool, which is when you, with all your strength, struck him in the head with the brick, causing him to sink back into the water unconscious, where he soon drowned. Since nobody else was home, it would naturally appear that he dove too deep and simply struck his head on the bottom of the pool. You might have even used the skimmer pole to position him just right before leaving. The brick went back in your handbag.

"But then just as you were getting ready to leave, Brian showed up with the can of dog food. He had brought the dog back earlier, but Connor then mentioned that he was out of dog food. Brian told him not to bother going out; he'd buy a can and bring it over on the way to his gig. The printout at the White Hen Pantry on Main Street shows that a thirteen-point-two-ounce can of Pedigree Beef Stew was purchased there at 7:52 p.m., and the clerk on duty remembers that it was bought by a young man who fits Brian's description.

"So there you were with a dead father-in-law in the pool and Brian at the door with a can of dog food. You had to think quickly. You told him that Ellen and Connor had changed plans; they were going away for the night, maybe her sick sister, whatever. At any rate, you claimed that since Brian had a gig, you and Kevin had agreed to take the dog for the night and you had already bought dog food. So you told Brian to just leave the can he bought on the kitchen table. But now what to do about Brian? You told him that since Kevin had gotten up early for the trip to New Hampshire, he was tired and had said he was going to bed early. But you weren't tired. In fact what you would like to do was go with Brian to his gig, listen to his band. But now what about the dog? Naturally, Brian agreed to take the dog for one more night. There was still time for the two of you to take him back to the condo in neighboring Danvers and make it to Brandy's in Beverly in time for the first set.

"The two of you drove back to Brian's place in separate cars, and after he had brought Cedric upstairs, you told him to put his bass and amp in your car. You had decided you'd stay for all four sets and you would drive him home at the end of the night. Flattered, Brian readily agreed.

"Then as you were driving through the wooded section on the way to Beverly, you lured Brian out of the car. Maybe pretended to have a mechanical problem or hear a strange noise coming from a tire, anything. Point is, you got him out of the car in a desolate area, and then as he was inspecting whatever the alleged problem was, you removed the brick from your handbag and used it for the second time that night. Only this time you used it more mercilessly. This time it didn't have to look like an accident. But now you had to get rid of the brick, so you quickly wiped it down and threw it into the woods. The handbag, you would take care of later.

"A few days later, after the police had conducted their preliminary investigation, you decided enough time had gone by and you couldn't take a chance on them checking out your car and verifying that Brian had been in it recently. So you contacted your buddy J.T. again. Hopefully he was more competent as a car thief than he was as a hit man."

Up to that point, Carol had let me deliver the entire account without interruption. For the most part she sat pallid and motionless, although I detected an occasional flash of rage in her eyes. When I was finished, she sat silent for a moment, still staring at me. Then when she opened her mouth to speak, nothing came out and she had to swallow and then clear her throat before beginning anew. Both her dry voice and her twisted smile trembled.

"Well that's quite a fabrication you've concocted," she tried. "But you're not a stupid man, Dean. I'm sure you can see that you've cut the puzzle pieces to make them fit. In fact I'm sure there are at least a half-dozen other scenarios that are equally viable." She arched her eyebrows defiantly, challenging me.

"Actually no," I said. "I ran through hundreds of possibilities, and I'm afraid that's the only one in which everything fits. And it also explains why you visited Toohig's condo after you closed the shop on Monday night."

This time the seething anger in her eyes was sustained. She was obviously outraged that I had followed her and there was no point in her trying to lie about it.

But then her brows arched in defiance again. "If you're so

sure about all this, why haven't you gone to the police?" she asked.

"Actually, Carol, I have." I looked at my watch. My account had taken longer than I had figured. "They were due here four minutes ago. I'm sure they'll be along any moment now. And like I said before, Toohig didn't make it here because he's a guest of Boston's finest as we speak. How far out on a limb do you think he'll go for you?"

If the ashen complexion, the dry voice, and the trembling jaw hadn't given her away, certainly the conspicuously absent question would have. Since Peter was running a bit late anyway, I thought I might as well ask it.

"I notice, Carol, that you haven't asked *why* I would believe that you wanted to kill your father-in-law. It seems to me that if you had been innocent, the absurdity of my basic premise would have been the first thing you would have pointed out."

Her eyes now reflected something beyond rage, perhaps beyond reason itself. I noticed too that her breathing appeared to have become labored; her chest was expanding more than normal on each inhalation. I had to go for the confession.

"You're a very beautiful woman, Carol. I suspect you've been hearing that for as far back as you can remember. And you undoubtedly learned at a very early age how far you could get with just your looks alone. In fact you never really needed anything else, did you? And in the end, that single fact proved to be your downfall.

"After you were married for a few years, your husband began to show more of an interest in things besides you. Not *instead* of you, but simply *besides* you. Sailing, friends, the establishment of his medical practice. A perfectly normal, healthy reaction, but unfortunately not one that you could cope with. Your father had died when you were only a child, and now you felt abandoned yet again by a man who was supposed to love you. Love you in a way that was humanly impossible.

"But then there was Connor. All he wanted was to be the father you no longer had. But you had other ideas. You needed to know that you could possess him totally. Probably partly to get even with your husband Kevin, and partly because you had something to prove to yourself.

"At any rate, you took that kind and decent man, and you did something reprehensible—you seduced him. Your own father-in-law. I don't know what moment of weakness you caught him in, but I'm sure he must have been going through something of his own at the time.

"Anyway, it went on for a while—you and he 'playing golf.' But finally, when he simply couldn't live with himself anymore, he did what he simply thought was the right thing. But you didn't think it was the right thing. You thought you had once again been abandoned, rejected. How dare he! Indeed how dare *any* man reject you on the basis of the very criterion by which you so wholly defined yourself!"

Carol opened her mouth and made one big gasp for air, but then, instead of fainting, she jumped up suddenly, taking me totally by surprise. With a rage that now possessed her entire being, she lifted the chair up over her head and, just as I became aware of what was happening, she began to bring it down upon me with the full force of her manic fury.

I'd barely had time to flinch when I saw a black and tan bundle of fur come flying into view from the left, knocking Carol over chair and all. As Cedric grabbed hold of her wrist and growled menacingly, I jumped up, grabbed one of her legs, twisted her onto her stomach and firmly planted a foot on the small of her back.

Carol began hyperventilating as a loud knock came at the door.

"Kick it in!" I shouted.

Two Salem police officers burst in with Peter, out of his jurisdiction, right behind them.

I looked at my watch. Then I looked up at Peter. "Why didn't you wait a little longer?"

"Hey, you complained that I'm always too early," he said. "Which way do you want it?"

Chapter 20

While Carol Bradley was being read her Miranda rights, I strolled off to the side and called Lieutenant Schmidlin. He arrived outside the bookstore just in time to see me being interviewed by the Channel 3 news team.

Peter explained that his tardiness had actually been the result of interdepartmental haggling. Both communication and coordination had taken longer than he'd expected.

Of course, technically, Carol hadn't yet admitted to the murders, but my account in conjunction with what was offered by Jason Toohig would be enough to get the DA to seek an indictment.

Later that night, Cedric took a well-deserved nap on the floor of the study while Nicole and I sipped our wine by the fireplace.

"Did the clerk at the convenience store really remember what the customer who bought a can of dog food looked like?" Nicole asked.

"Nah."

"I didn't think so." She took a sip of her wine. "What do you think makes a man as righteous as Connor Bradley go so far astray?"

"I'd ask Dr. Meier, but I'm going broke buying him wine."

"I'm sure Feldman will want me to do a human interest story on the case. After it airs I don't think you'll have to worry about going broke for a while."

"Well I'm not going to worry about buying Meier wine either. Besides, the real hero is asleep on the floor here."

She took another sip and thought hard before asking the next question. "It was such a radical idea—a well-respected doctor and upstanding citizen like Connor Bradley having an affair with his own daughter-in-law. How did you ever think of that?"

"I must be as perverse as he was."

"No, really," she insisted.

"Well you always hear that the two biggest motives for murder are money and passion. Schmidlin had it right; the money angle didn't fit from any direction. It had to be passion. But then, having gotten that far, he took the more logical route—the wife and Golden. That wasn't a bad theory, but there were still things that didn't fit. Fortunately, Schmidlin wasn't able to think out of the box as they say. And come to think of it, neither was I, at least not consciously. It was the little man who figured it out."

Nicole smiled at me. "So Cedric is the 'real hero' and the little man in your brain gets the credit for solving the puzzle. Why, Dean Cello, do you sell yourself short? Why can't you take any of the credit that you so rightfully deserve?"

"You're right," I said. "I'm a freakin' genius. Want to sleep with me?"

Despite the fact that it ended up being a long, passionate night, Cedric and I were up at our usual time to run the next morning. We did the regular route along the esplanade. When we got back, I sat with him on the floor of the study and told him the good news—"It's you and me, pal." It seemed that he was laughing. As if he'd known all along.

A couple of days later, Ellen Bradley called and invited both Nicole and me to tea. When we arrived, Dr. Golden was already there. Ellen served the tea in her formal room and expressed her "deepest appreciation" for my having solved the murders of her husband and nephew. At one point in the conversation, Dr. Golden mentioned that the two of them were planning a trip to the Bahamas in two weeks. Ellen's comment was, "Well after all, we're not getting any younger." Before we left, I gave Ellen the $100 candlestick holders. I told her I thought they'd look nice on her Sorrento teacart. What did I know?

As we were driving back toward the city, Nicole asked, "Whose infidelity do you think came first?"

"We'll never know," was the best I could do.

The next Monday morning, while I was reading the sports page, Dr. Benjamin Meier called to congratulate me on my successful solving of the Bradley murders.

"While I have you doctor… a well-respected educated man with an established practice taking up with his daughter-in-law. What would cause such an intelligent and otherwise decent man to do such a thing?"

"Mr. Cello, I'm sure you've heard that anyone, under the right circumstances, is capable of murder. Do you find infidelity even *more* egregious?"

I thought before answering. If I were to be honest, in a way a sexual relationship with one's daughter-in-law… But I didn't want the good doctor to suggest that I should be consulting him on a more personal basis. "You make a good point, Doctor."

"That's one in the bank for me, right? My wife enjoys a good Chablis."

How could you not like this guy?

I put down the phone and looked at Cedric. Simply out of curiosity, I went to the desk and added up all the expenses I'd incurred working on the Bradley case. To my surprise, they worked out to only about $430. I had looked in the *Sunday Globe* and noted that Airedale pups ranged from $800 to $1100, and those little guys and gals were not yet champions. I decided I didn't want to know whether or not Ellen Bradley had placed a stop payment on her husband's check. I would save it as a memento. I had, after all, already been paid quite handsomely. And the plethora of new cases soon to come would be icing on the cake.

I was just getting up from the desk when the phone rang again.

"Good morning, Mr. Cello. This is Chuck at Commonwealth Motors. You'll be pleased to know that your car is ready, sir."

I realized that I wasn't all that pleased. In fact, I hadn't even missed it.

"How much do you want for the old Volvo I've got?"

Before the day was out Chuck and I worked out a deal that was agreeable to both of us. I had never really been the stud type anyway.

On Tuesday night of the following week, Peter and I met for dinner at High Tide. I arrived five minutes early and, of course, he was already there.

"Another Volvo?" he smirked. "When are you going back to school teaching?"

"The day after you start feeding and mowing the lawn."

He looked at me.

"Guess I'm safe for awhile, huh?"

Two weeks after the arrest of Carol Bradley, Nicole was on assignment down in Newport one night, so I ate a frozen pizza, watched the ballgame, took Cedric to the corner and back, and then went to bed.

My eyes had been closed for less than a minute when they suddenly popped wide open again. Did the little man in my brain never rest? I heard several of Nicole's comments play back simultaneously—"What style wedding dress... You're welcome to join me in Derry... I just love... fences... porches." It wasn't really about Cape Cod fences and front porches, was it?

Printed in the United States
80275LV00001B/208-300

9 781587 368264